The Con Artist

Be careful who you trust...

Victoria Webster

Grosvenor House
Publishing Limited

This book is published by
Grosvenor House Publishing Ltd
Link House
140 The Broadway, Tolworth, Surrey, KT6 7HT.
www.grosvenorhousepublishing.co.uk

A CIP catalogue record for this book
is available from the British Library.

ISBN 978-1-80381-153-6
eBook ISBN 978-1-80381-154-3

PART ONE

MITCH AND MARNIE

Mitch and Marnie were standing in the living room of their small suburban bungalow.

'Now, Marnie, you know what you've got to do? Don't deviate from the plan and everything will go smoothly. Don't force the tears. They'll come naturally enough. Is that clear?'

Marnie nodded her head dolefully. 'Yes, Mitch, but it seems dishonest. What has she ever done to us?'

'She's done nothing, but she's just got divorced and her ex-husband is wealthy, so I'm assuming she got a generous divorce settlement. I did a search on one of those satellite Earth maps to see where she's moved to and it's obvious she lives in an affluent area. Most of the houses have swimming pools, large driveways and substantial gardens, so she's not short of a bob or two. Listen, Marnie,' said Mitch, pointing his finger at her, 'we're in a bit of a pickle here. It's sink or swim, and I'm not about to sink. Is that clear?'

'Yes, Mitch, it's clear. What time will the men arrive?'

'You don't need to know that. That way, there'll be an element of surprise. Right, I'm off. Ring me as arranged. Just remember – keep calm and keep cool.'

With Mitch's remark hanging in the air, he was off, leaving Marnie with a bundle of misgivings and a bag of ragged nerves.

VICKY

Vicky didn't know why she was doing this. Her weekend had been planned for some time, but here she was sitting in traffic on the M1 having already spent two hours in a solid queue on the M25. Vicky's problem was that she was too soft-hearted, with a tendency to hold onto feelings of loyalty to people and places which she long ceased to have any connection with. Yes, it was true, she had spent many happy childhood summers with her aunt and uncle, and her cousin, Mitch. However, that was a long, long time ago and, apart from the exchange of birthday and Christmas cards, containing the barest of news, contact was minimal. Still, her cousin had been quite forceful on the telephone.

'You must come to Mum's 80th birthday party,' he had said. 'It's a surprise and she'll be delighted to see you.'

'I can't,' Vicky had replied. 'I've already made plans, and also it's a long way to come and Friday is probably just about the worst day to travel up North.'

'I'm not taking no for an answer, Cousin Vicky. Family is family.' And here Mitch employed emotional blackmail. 'Mum hasn't been well. This might be her last birthday, and your last chance to see her. We've made a special film for her of her life, and you're in it. Do you remember all those happy summers we spent together?'

So, this was why Vicky found herself travelling up North on a busy Friday morning, feeling very put out.

MARNIE

Marnie was waiting anxiously for Vicky to arrive. She had checked everything over and over again. The piles of money, which were actually photocopies of a ten-pound note which Mitch had carefully cut out, and then placed a real note on top of each pile, were laid out in rows on the table. Framed photographs were dotted around the room. Some were in colour showing Mitch and Marnie on holiday, family shots of Mitch and his mum, Catherine, and dad, Clifford, who had died many years ago, and a black and white photograph of Vicky and Mitch as children standing in front of the family home. Marnie looked around the room. Everything was in its place, and if she was asked to describe the house, she would say it looked thoroughly respectable, and very ordinary. Marnie's mobile rang, making her jump. It was Vicky ringing to say she was about 30 minutes away.

*

Vicky pulled up outside a small, detached bungalow which had a pocket handkerchief front garden with a neat border of colourful flowers. A front doormat declared "WELCOME". Before Vicky had time to ring the bell, the door was opened by a smiling woman who embraced Vicky warmly.

'Come in, come in. How are you? How was your journey? What time did you set off?' gabbled the woman.

This, thought Vicky, *must be Marnie.* Not having seen her for over 20 years, with only the occasional

5

photograph, Vicky had forgotten what Marnie looked like, and thought that she seemed nervous; or perhaps she was just naturally effusive. In any event, Vicky felt verbally assaulted. A memory came flooding back of her first impressions of the woman when she had married Mitch – an alliteration of plump, plain and pleasant – dressed in a bright white wedding dress with a full skirt which, Vicky had thought at the time, reminded her of a meringue. Her second impression, having now seen her again, was no more favourable than the first. Wearing stretch black leggings, and a red shapeless blouse made from flimsy material, she was still clearly overweight. As to her hairstyle, *why, oh why, oh why,* thought Vicky, *did women who had round, plump faces always have their hair cut very short which only emphasised their big cheeks?* Her cousin, Mitch, on the other hand, was handsome; not strikingly handsome enough to make him memorable, but very easy on the eye and certainly charming. Again, Vicky had wondered at the time what her cousin had seen in the woman he was marrying. Almost immediately, Vicky felt guilty at having such negative thoughts, particularly as Marnie had welcomed her so warmly and was now taking off Vicky's coat and ushering her into the living room.

As Marnie disappeared into the kitchen to make tea, Vicky surveyed the small living room. The interior was like walking into a garden centre. Flowered carpet, flowered settee and chairs, and flowered curtains. *Blimey,* she thought, *it's like a "Britain in Bloom" competition.* The furniture consisted of a coffee table in dark wood, two matching side tables, a dining table and chairs which – somewhat refreshingly, she thought – were covered in plain fabric. There was nothing ostensibly wrong with the interior, reflected Vicky, but it was all a bit generically boring and lacking in imagination. Vicky also noticed the piles of ten-pound notes on the top of the table. She thought it was odd but dismissed it for the time being.

From the kitchen, Marnie had been furtively glancing at her visitor. She hadn't seen Cousin Vicky for at least 20 years, and that had been on her wedding day. Revelling in being the centre of attention for once, she had paid little attention to those guests on Mitch's side of the family who had been invited. She had seen Mitch hugging an attractive blonde, who she didn't recognise, and had gone over to them.

'Ah, Marnie,' Mitch had said, 'meet by beautiful cousin, Vicky. Vicky, meet the wife, Mrs Marnie Mitchelson.'

Later that evening, Marnie had said, 'Well, if she's so beautiful, how come she hasn't netted a husband yet?'

Mitch had replied, 'Vicky throws more back in than she keeps. She's waiting for the big catch, just like the one you landed.' And then he had laughed.

Coming back to the present, Marnie thought to herself that Vicky may have landed her "big catch", to use Mitch's words, but that "catch" had thrown Vicky back in. *There she is*, Marnie thought to herself, *wearing perfectly fitting jeans, and a pink and white striped blouse with the collar turned up, just like those female presenters on morning television*. Marnie also noticed that Vicky's hair was styled in a perfect bob with completely straight edges and not a hair out of place. Her own hair was kept short. She cut the sides and fringe herself, whilst Mitch kept the back tidy, and so she had no need to go to a hairdresser, which, in Mitch's view, was a waste of money. She also took in Vicky's compact quilted handbag with a discreet logo on the front, which Marnie had no doubt was a designer bag. *But*, thought Marnie, *I've got something she hasn't. She hasn't got a husband, and I have.* With that, Marnie picked up the tray of tea and biscuits and proudly walked into the living room, plonking the tray down on the coffee table. 'Shall I be mum?' she asked.

Before Vicky could answer, Marnie began to dig a deep hole for herself. 'I was so sorry to hear of your divorce, Vicky. It must be hard on you, seeing as you were together for so many years and that he left you for another woman, and an older one, at that. And you being so lovely and taking care of yourself, it just doesn't make sense to me and Mitch.' Marnie, oblivious to the surprised look on Vicky's face at such an outburst, took a sip of tea and bit into a chocolate biscuit.

That's right, thought Vicky, *stuff your chubby face,* and then immediately felt mean.

Marnie ploughed on regardless. 'I don't know what I would do if I caught Mitch cheating, but then again, when we married, we took our vows seriously. Love, honour and obey, for richer and poorer...' And at this point, Marnie stopped as she remembered the mess they were currently in and saw that Vicky had gone red in the face and very quiet. Marnie realised she had spoken too bluntly. 'Anyway, here I am blathering on. Me and Mitch are very grateful to you for giving up your weekend to come to Cath's party. It will mean so much to her.'

Vicky, who was feeling irritated by Marnie's insensitive remarks, but chose to let them go over her head, replied, 'It's no problem, Marnie. I had organised my weekend already, but, as Mitch reminded me, "family is family". Also, Uncle Clifford and Aunty Cath were always very kind to me when I came to stay, so it's the least I can do.'

Both women fell silent, each sipping their tea and eating the biscuits. Vicky was quietly asking herself why in God's name had she agreed to come. In a short space of time, and with the benefit of hindsight, she would look back on that day and kick herself for uttering those fateful five words, "Have you lived here long?"

Marnie, on the other hand, was silently panicking as Plan A was not exactly going as planned, and there wasn't a Plan B in place. Just then, Vicky asked, 'Have you lived here long?'

Bingo, thought Marnie, *Plan A is back on,* and she nearly punched the air, but restrained herself.

'The reason I ask is because I used to have a different address for you, and I thought you lived in the country rather than in the town.'

'We used to live in a small village but found it too claustrophobic. Everyone knew everyone else's business, so we moved here. Also, it's much nearer to the care home where Cath now lives.'

'Oh, I see. Well, that must be convenient for you both.'

On her way in, Vicky had noticed that many of the shops were boarded up, and the general area looked to be run down. This prompted her to ask if things were okay for the two of them, as the move here seemed to indicate a downwards move if the house they had previously lived in, from the solitary photograph she had, was anything to go by.

Marnie now felt on firmer ground. Leaning forward slightly in the chair, and placing both hands palm down on her knees, she looked Vicky in the face and replied, 'Well, since you ask, I'm going to be frank with you. We've lived here for a while, but not entirely from choice. When Mitch's business was doing well, before the recession, we lived in a much bigger house – which I believe Mitch sent you a photograph of – in a village about 10 miles from here. That would be the address you had. But needs must and when money got tight, we cut our cloth, so to speak. We sold the house, paid off some of the mortgage and downsized to this bungalow. However, things still aren't back to normal. The housing market is still in a slump, which means the building trade hasn't picked up, so there's not much call at the moment for plant and machinery hire. Mitch won't have told you this, but he's currently employed on a zero-hour contract with a parcel delivery firm and also works part-time for a DIY store, which also isn't doing too great at the moment.'

At this point, Marnie took a breath and sat back in the chair, placing her hands in her lap. 'As for me, I had a job with BHS in the town centre, but that closed down and then I managed to get a few hours with a concession in House of Fraser, but I've been made redundant because the concession also closed. So, to be honest with you, Vicky, we're in a bit of a mess. We're in the red with the bank, and have an overdraft, and in arrears with the mortgage, so it's looking likely the house will be repossessed. So, there you have it.'

Vicky was shocked to hear all of this. 'I'm sorry to hear this, Marnie. I had no idea things were so bad.'

'Well, why would you? Me and Mitch try not bother people with our troubles, especially family. And you've had troubles of your own to contend with, I imagine.' As Mitch had directed her to do, Marnie fell silent and lowered her head as if in shame. When she eventually looked up, she whispered, 'We owe £30,000.'

'£30,000!' shrieked Vicky. 'Crikey, that's a lot of debt.' As if on cue, and much to Marnie's delight, Vicky continued, 'But, Marnie, I can't help noticing, what's all that money on the table?'

Marnie could hear Mitch's voice in her head, saying *right, Marnie, reel her in, nice and slow. You're about to land a big catch.*

'That,' said Marnie, 'is money we owe to a certain person. £10,000 and it's got to be paid in cash. The person we owe the money to isn't the type you don't repay.' Marnie leant forward in her chair, and in hushed tones said, 'He's a loan shark.'

'Loan shark!' shouted Vicky, quite taken aback. 'What on earth have you and Mitch got yourselves involved in?'

Marnie shrugged her shoulders. 'These things happen, Vicky. And the rest of the money we owe to the bank and the mortgage provider.'

Before Vicky could respond, there was a loud banging on the front door, which made both women jump. Marnie rose up from the chair and went to answer the door. Vicky could hear deep male voices, and then the door to the living room opened and two well-built, shaven-headed, men entered, dressed all in black. Although Marnie asked them to take a seat, they said they preferred standing and went on to introduce themselves as Dale and Dean from DCA debt collection agency. Dale, who was the larger of the two in height and weight, and clearly senior, announced to Marnie in an authoritative tone, 'We have a warrant of execution to recover a debt of £10,000 today, and we are instructed by our client, Bricks and Mortar Limited, not to leave without payment in full. We could, of course, remove goods to the value of, but looking around, Mrs Mitchelson, and please don't be offended, I don't think there's much of value here. Certainly not enough to clear the debt.'

'There's no need to be rude,' said Vicky, suddenly feeling defensive on Marnie's behalf.

'Excuse me, madam, but I don't believe I am being rude. And you are?'

'I'm Victoria, Mr Mitchelson's cousin. You can't just barge in here demanding money.'

'I don't believe we did barge in, madam,' said Dean. 'Mrs Mitchelson invited us in, and we have every right to ask for the money owed to our client. We have a legal document from the court instructing us to recover this debt today.'

Marnie fell back into the chair and put her head in her hands, sighing loudly. Removing her hands from her face, she looked up at the two debt collectors in despair. 'I don't know what to do. Can I ring my husband?'

'Yes of course, Mrs Mitchelson,' said Dale. 'In the meantime, Dean will start listing goods but, as I said...'

Marnie picked up her mobile that was lying on the table and pretended to call Mitch. 'He's not picking up. I don't know what to do.' Marnie was now beginning to feel genuinely agitated because Mitch hadn't fully prepared her for the visit from the men.

'Marnie,' Vicky said, 'what about the money on the table? There's enough money, surely, to pay off this debt now and then these *gentlemen*,' and Vicky emphasised the word "gentlemen", 'can be on their way.'

'That's not possible,' replied Marnie curtly. 'That money, as you know, belongs to someone else, and it would be more than Mitch's life was worth to give that away.'

Marnie put her head in her hands again and began to cry. Her crying was genuine, as she was beginning to find the lies and deception completely overwhelming. Recovering slightly, she pretended to phone Mitch again. 'Mitch, it's Marnie. I've got two debt collectors here. They're after £10,000 today, or else they're going to take our possessions. What shall I do?'

...

'Oh, okay, give them the money on the table? Right, and what do we do about the person we owe that money to?'

...

'Oh, okay. Yes, I see.' Marnie got up and walked over to the table. Scooping up the bundles of paper, making sure the real ten-pound notes on the top were clearly on show, she handed the whole lot to Dale and Dean. After signing a receipt for the money, she showed the two men out. When she returned, she flopped back down on the chair and put her head in her hands once again.

*

On the day Vicky's husband, Howard, came home and announced that he had met someone else and wanted a divorce, Vicky's response was not 'You cheating bastard,' or 'Who is she? I'll scratch her eyes out!' or 'I'll take you for every penny you've got,' but a plaintive, 'But why, Howie? What have I done?'

Howie might have replied, 'Because you've put on weight' (which wasn't the case, although she had put on a few pounds), or 'because you've become boring and stuck in your ways' (which might be partially true). Instead, his response was, 'Because, Vicky, you're too easy going, and uncomplaining. You need to be more demanding and high maintenance. More Jimmy Choo, less Freeman Hardy and Willis (at this last comment, Vicky felt that Howard – who was a few years older than her – was showing his age). Also, you're too kind and fall for any old sob story, and then people take advantage of you.' Which is why Vicky found herself sitting with a distraught Marnie, offering her £30,000 to get her cousin and his wife out of a financial hole.

Marnie flapped her hands, and then put them over her mouth, then removed them before saying, 'But how will you do that? How?'

Vicky sighed. 'If I go into town now, I might just make the bank before it closes. I'll withdraw £10,000 in cash to replace the money on the table and transfer the remainder to your bank account over the weekend. It'll have to be done in two lots, possibly three, but the money should arrive in your account by Tuesday. Wednesday at the latest. You just need to give me your bank details.'

'I don't know what to say, Vicky. This is most kind of you.'

'To be honest, Marnie, this has all come as a bit of a shock. I didn't realise things were so bad, and I found it quite alarming to have those two men here. I'm going to the bank now, and then I'm going to my hotel to have a lie down. I'll come back in the morning with the money, and then I'll get changed for the party in the afternoon.'

'You're an angel, Vicky. How can we ever repay you for your kindness? Mitch always said you were one of the best and his favourite cousin.' She kissed Vicky on both cheeks and ushered her quickly out of the door. As Marnie stood on the doorstep, smiling and waving Vicky goodbye, Vicky got into her red Mercedes SLK feeling very put out and intuitively sensing that something was amiss but couldn't pin down exactly what.

Returning to the living room, the first thing Marnie did, after pouring a ready-mixed gin and tonic to steady her nerves, was to phone Mitch.

'She's gone, Mitch. She fell for it. I feel awful, I really do, but it's obvious she's not short of money if her car is anything to go by. You can come back now, and I'll tell you all about it.'

Mitch, who had been in the pub at the end of the road, where he had been waiting for his friends, Dale and Dean, to give them some money as payment for their "acting" role, which they subsequently lost in the bookmakers, finished his beer and walked back to the bungalow.

*

After a restless night in the hotel where Vicky was staying, she had breakfast and then set out to see Marnie and Mitch with the money. She had rung to say that she was on her way and would see them shortly. Mitch made a quick exit, whilst Marnie cut up a large onion to make her eyes water so that when she opened the door it would look as if she'd been crying.

Pulling up outside the bungalow, Vicky stepped out of her Mercedes and walked up the path. As if on cue, the door opened to reveal a red-eyed Marnie, who was in the process of wiping them with her fingers.

'Whatever is wrong, Marnie? You look as if you've been crying. You don't need to worry now. I've got the money here, and the rest is being transferred.'

'Oh, Vicky,' wailed Marnie, 'Cath had a stroke in the night and was taken to hospital but sadly passed away this morning. Mitch has been at the hospital for hours, so at least she didn't die alone.'

'Oh my God, that's awful. Can I do anything? Perhaps I should go to the hospital and see Mitch.'

'No, no, don't do that. He'll have such a lot to do and he's in shock at the moment. I think the best thing, and I'm sorry you've come all this way, is for you to go home. We'll contact you as soon as we've organised the funeral.'

'Okay, well if you're sure. I suppose that probably is the best course of action. Look, here's the £10,000. The remainder should be in your account within the next few days. Give my love to Mitch.' After giving Marnie a quick hug, Vicky walked back to her car and drove away, thinking that what she had experienced in such a short space of time was nothing short of mind-boggling.

Mitch, who had been hiding around the back of the bungalow, came in through the kitchen door. 'Right, Marnie, get packing.'

'Where are we going?' she asked.

'You're going to Luton. I'm going down south.'

PART TWO

DOROTHY

Dorothy was having her usual Wednesday coffee morning with her friends from the local church. 'I'm thinking about taking in a lodger,' she announced to the group. 'With George gone, I'm missing male company. So, I thought I'd advertise for someone who is looking for lodgings during the week, and who goes home at the weekend. That would suit me perfectly.'

'You'd better watch out, Dorothy. You might get yourself a toy boy as a lodger,' said Marjorie Walker, with a wink.

'Get away with you. I'm too old for that,' replied Dorothy laughing.

'Oh, you're never too old if everything is still in working order,' piped up Eunice Stokes, which caused some of the group to splutter into their coffee.

So it was that, a week later, Dorothy advertised in her local paper, the *Saltdean News*, and in the window of her local newsagent, for a lodger who was looking for bed and breakfast, Monday to Friday. Enquiries to Mrs Dorothy Beresford, and she listed her landline number. References, of course, would be required.

MITCH

Mitch had always fancied the south-east coast but hadn't a clue where to begin. Spreading a map of Sussex out on the kitchen table of their rented one-bedroom flat in one of the many high-density backstreets of Luton, he was drawn to the coastal resort of Brighton in East Sussex. He had never been to Brighton but enjoyed reading the crime novels written by Peter James whose stories were set in Brighton and vividly brought the area to life. He had also seen numerous television programmes which had featured Brighton Pier and the pebbly beach. There was also, he had read somewhere, a disreputable side to the place and Mitch felt instinctively drawn there.

The map showed how spread out and sprawling the general area was. In one direction was Hove, which appeared to be a continuum of Brighton, followed by Southwick and then Shoreham. In the opposite direction, the area became less developed. The map showed Brighton Marina on the right-hand side adjacent to the sea, and then on the other side of the coastal road there was a green area which was a golf course, with houses set back from the course. The village of Rottingdean looked to be a self-contained location, and then the area began to become more built-up in Saltdean and Peacehaven.

Having got a general idea of the area from the map, Mitch then logged onto one of the well-known property websites to search for affluent areas in Brighton. He had conducted a similar search for Luton, which is how he had found the cheap rental property where Marnie was now living. Starting with houses for sale, with the most expensive showing first, he was able to see which locations in Brighton attracted the wealthy, and it would be these areas where he would look for his next target. *Simples*, he said to himself. His next task was to find somewhere temporary to stay in Brighton, which he would use as a base whilst he looked for longer-term lodgings. Typing in "Bed and Breakfast accommodation", a long list popped up. He wasn't concerned with reviews; something cheap and hopefully cheerful would suffice and if it had a sea view, then that was a bonus. A further search revealed that many of the B & Bs had vacancies, so he decided to take a chance and book into one once he was there.

A couple of hours later, after telling Marnie to keep her head down and not draw attention to herself, he kissed her on the cheek, bid her adieu and headed down south.

*

Chris Rea was singing about the "Road to Hell" which, felt Mitch, perfectly summed up the congested M25. Soon the sign for the M23 came into view, and he took the turning off the M25. The traffic was a bit lighter – but only just – and then he was on the A27 heading towards Brighton. Crossing a large, busy roundabout, he drove through somewhere called Patcham and then followed a slightly confusing one-way system. Luckily, he had a TomTom affixed to his windscreen, but still found the navigation difficult to follow because there were so many side roads and a lot of building work was taking place which meant road closures and diversions. Passing Brighton Pavilion and then a small park on the right-hand side, he headed towards the seafront. He took a right turn at a small roundabout, noting that Rottingdean was sign-posted left, and drove along the front. Prior to starting his trip, he had programmed in an address for a B & B that fitted his criteria. It directed him to take a right turn into a narrow road just off the seafront and instructed him to stop outside an undistinguished-looking terraced house with a board bearing the words "Sunnyside Up Bed and Breakfast. Vacancies. En Suite. Wi-Fi."

The house appeared to be well-looked-after, with no peeling paintwork, and two hanging baskets with colourful flowers hung either side of the door. Deciding that he would stay here, rather than drive around looking at other places, his luck was in when he saw a parking space nearby. It was a "pay at meter" space, and Mitch was shocked when he saw the cost for one hour and began to have second thoughts. Checking to see if there were any traffic wardens lurking nearby, he didn't put any money into the meter in case he decided not to stay there. He rang the doorbell and was buzzed in. He was greeted by a middle-aged man who introduced himself as Kenneth, the proprietor. Mitch mentioned the cost of parking and was relieved when Kenneth said that he would give him parking vouchers for the length of his stay. Then, with a theatrical gesture, he threw his hands up in the air and said to Mitch, 'My dear, these wardens are such a nightmare. Now go put that voucher in your car, get your bags and I'll show you to your delightful room.'

Mitch's room was on the second floor. There was no sea view, but it was clean and furnished with evident care, although it was not to Mitch's taste. Two chairs, one upholstered in grey crushed velvet and the other in the same fabric but the colour pink, were placed either side of a round table which had a mosaic design of two nude men standing either side of a Grecian urn on the table-top. The double bed had white bedding, with two lime green scatter cushions placed neatly against the white pillowcases. For Mitch, it was all a bit garish but the main thing was that it was reasonably priced, and he wasn't going to stay there very long anyway.

After unpacking, he set up his laptop and conducted an initial search for people looking for a lodger. There were too many advertisements, and they were mixed in with information about bed and breakfast accommodation, guest houses and hostels. Deciding that it would be too time-consuming to sift through them all, and the cost and time involved in making phone calls and driving around the busy streets to do viewings, he decided he would look outside of the immediate Brighton area where it would be less touristy.

Having not eaten since breakfast, he was hungry. He shut down his laptop and went out in search of food. The weather was nice, and he took a stroll along the seafront in the direction of Hove. He passed by two iconic Brighton landmarks: the skeleton of the original pier, which looked as if it was about to topple into the sea, and The Grand Hotel on the opposite side of the road. Spotting two restaurants that were next to each other on the same side as hotel, with the one on the corner having outside seating, he crossed over the road and chose the one with tables outside and sat down. Mitch always associated the seaside with fish and chips, and so that was what he ordered. He thought the cost of the wine was exorbitant, and so ordered a lager. He hadn't realised that Brighton would be so expensive compared to resorts in Yorkshire such as Bridlington or Scarborough. Having satisfied his hunger, he walked back to the B & B feeling upbeat, and excited about his new batch of "projects".

When Mitch woke up the next morning, he had a good feeling. On entering the breakfast room, he noticed that all the guests were male. Whilst some reminded him of well-built truck drivers, others were dressed in brightly coloured lycra and looked very fit. Mitch concluded, therefore, that they must be on a cycling tour although he hadn't seen any bicycles. He was also aware that he was attracting some appraising looks. The penny dropped when Kenneth came in and asked, 'Who would like a big sausage for breakfast?' All hands shot up, including Mitch's. He was many things, but homophobic he was not, and he found the banter and irreverence that followed added to his high spirits. After breakfast, he returned to his room and gathered together the belongings he would need for the day.

As Mitch stepped outside, he was greeted by sunshine and lamented the fact that he couldn't take the day off for another walk along the seafront. Today, however, was a day of exploration and he set off in his car. He drove around the residential roads in Brighton, taking note of those areas with large properties. Next, he drove back along the seafront and passed Brighton Pier and Brighton Sea Life Centre on his right, and then came to the small roundabout and headed towards Rottingdean. He passed the marina on his right, and then the golf course with a café on his left. An imposing building, set back on the left, turned out to be Roedean School, with a windmill further along acting as a second landmark. At the traffic lights, he turned left into the village of Rottingdean. The high street contained a sprinkling of shops, a number of cafés and two pubs. For such a small place, it was very congested with traffic and only having partial pavements for pedestrians, many of whom were elderly, and young mothers with pushchairs, they were forced to walk in the road. Having driven through the village, he passed a bowling green on his left and then that seemed to be the end of Rottingdean. Deciding that

Rottingdean would be too small a place in which to lodge, because as a newcomer he would be conspicuous, he turned the car around and headed back through the village, turning left at the lights and drove towards Saltdean.

As the map had shown, Saltdean was more built-up than Rottingdean, with a network of roads stretching back from the seafront. Saltdean could not be described as a village, or a town. Nevertheless, it still had the feel of a community. Not being familiar with the area, he drove around until he came to a road with a variety of shops and businesses on either side. Parking was no problem, so he pulled over and decided to go for a walk and explore. Passing a newsagent's shop, he bought a copy of the *Saltdean News* and decided to get a coffee in a café he had just passed. However, his eye was caught by a noticeboard in the newsagent's window advertising local matters. He saw a postcard with the heading "Lodger Wanted", which had been put up by a Mrs Dorothy Beresford, who was looking for a weekday lodger. Breakfast was included. References would be required. Mrs Beresford had listed her landline number.

VICKY

Ten days after Vicky's trip up North, she woke up one morning and realised that she had heard nothing further about Aunty Cath's funeral, nor indeed had any communication whatsoever from Mitch or Marnie. She had, as promised, transferred the remaining £20,000, and was surprised not to have received a phone call thanking her. Instead, there had been total silence. Picking up her mobile, she dialled Marnie's number, and was informed that the number was no longer in use. So, she dialled Mitch's number, and received the same reply. *How odd*, she thought, but reflected on how the whole experience and drama of the situation had been odd. She remembered Marnie's gushing welcome, which she now thought seemed more like nervousness, the piles of money on the table which had seemed strange at the time, and the random photograph of her and Mitch as children. Now, with the benefit of hindsight, the whole thing seemed like a stage set with props for a suburban "kitchen sink" drama. *That can't be right, though,* she thought, and she relived the arrival of Dale and Dean, the two debt collectors. Vicky watched the TV programmes, *The Sheriffs are Coming* and *Can't Pay We'll Take It Away*, so she knew that the scenario she had witnessed happened in real life, so it must have been real. *Or was it?* she now asked herself. Nevertheless, something wasn't right. Which is why she found herself driving up the M25 on her way to the M1 to see Mitch and Marnie – again.

MITCH

'**H**ello. Is that Mrs Beresford? Dorothy Beresford?'

'Yes, that's correct.'

'Good morning. My name is Daniel Simpson and I'm calling about your advertisement for a lodger.'

'Oh, I didn't expect to get a response so quickly. You are aware it's only Monday to Friday?'

'Monday to Friday is fine, as I go home to my wife and son at the weekend.'

'Ah, that's perfect. Do you have any idea how long you would need the room for?'

'No, I don't know how long I'll be needing somewhere to stay, as I'm working on a contract in Newhaven, and it depends on how long the project will take to finish. I'm sure it will be for a few months, if that's okay, as I don't want to waste your time.'

'That will suit me fine, Mr Simpson. By the way, do you smoke?'

'No, I don't smoke, Mrs Beresford, and I don't keep late hours either. Are you free for me to come and see the room now?'

*

Mitch started the car and put on the TomTom. The screen showed a network of roads, and he found himself gradually going up into the hilly part of Saltdean. Pulling up outside the number of the house he had been given, he took in the larger than average and well-maintained bungalow, which had leaded windows and two conical shaped plants placed either side of the entrance. An orange-coloured rectangular doormat bore the words "WELCOME" written in large black letters. Mitch rang the doorbell, and a woman who looked to be in her mid- to late-60s – although he thought it was difficult to tell a person's age these days – answered the door. She was wearing a knitted cream twin set, over a brown plaid skirt, and cream sandals. A gold and pearl necklace, and matching earrings, completed the tasteful and genteel look the woman presented. *Thank heavens she's not one of those older women who dress far too young for their age, and are plastered with make-up,* he thought with some relief, knowing that if she was one of those women he might be on the receiving end of unwanted attention.

Mitch extended his hand with an open smile. 'You must be Mrs Beresford? I'm Daniel. Pleased to meet you.'

'Hello, Daniel. Pleased to meet you too. Do come in, and I'll show you the room you'll be staying in if you decide to take it. Oh, and you can call me Dorothy.'

Dorothy took the man she knew as Daniel to the back of the bungalow and showed him into a large bedroom which looked out onto the garden. She explained that the room was en-suite, with a shower, and if he wanted a bath there was the main bathroom just down the hallway. Mitch genuinely liked the room. It was light and airy, had a nice view of the garden, and looked very comfortable.

'If you'll have me, Dorothy, then I'll take it,' said Mitch with a smile.

'Of course I'll have you, Daniel,' replied Dorothy blushing slightly, as it took her back to the day when George had proposed to her: "If you'll have me, Dorothy, will you marry me?" Dorothy had replied, "Of course I'll have you, George." Coming back to the present, she said, 'Now, let's have some tea and we can discuss the small matter of rent and what you have for breakfast.'

She asked that he pay one month's rent in advance, which she explained was the norm, and also if he could provide her with at least two references. 'Oh, there's one thing I should have told you. I hope it won't be a problem, but I don't have any internet connection here. In fact, I don't even own a computer. My friends are always saying I need to get with the times, but I'm a bit of a dinosaur when it comes to technology.'

'Don't worry, Dorothy. I can connect to the internet using my mobile, and I can always use an internet café if need be. There seem to be plenty around.'

'Well, that's settled, then. When would you like to move in?'

'Would the day after tomorrow be okay with you? I don't have many belongings, so shall we say 10am?'

Dorothy confirmed that would be fine with her, and she waved Daniel goodbye feeling very pleased with herself. She couldn't wait to tell her friends that she had found a lodger who was handsome, very presentable and polite, just like her dear departed George.

THE CON ARTIST

VICKY

Vicky had a disquieting feeling in the pit of her stomach. She had tried to distract herself from her nagging thoughts whilst driving by listening to LBC and had heard yet another caller supporting Brexit, which annoyed her so much she switched to a music channel. The song being played was "Things Can Only Get Better" by D:Ream. *I bloody hope so*, she shouted out loud, but instinctively she knew that things were probably going to get worse.

A while later, she pulled up outside the bungalow which now had a "For Rent" sign in the front garden. It occurred to her that perhaps Mitch and Marnie had decided to rent out their home and move into a flat, which would ease their financial situation. *However, if this was the case*, she asked herself, *why haven't they forwarded their new address?* The "For Rent" board gave the name and telephone number of the estate agent, which meant that they would have a forwarding address.

Calling the number on the board, Vicky introduced herself and enquired as to the owners – Mr and Mrs Mitchelson. She asked if they had left a forwarding address, and when exactly they had left. The agent informed her that the owners of the property lived elsewhere, and Mr and Mrs Mitchelson were only tenants in the property. Furthermore, they had left suddenly without giving any notice, and had owed rent money, which they were very behind with. One positive thing about them, the agent told Vicky, was that they had left the place clean and tidy and had looked after the garden. 'You wouldn't believe the mess some tenants leave the properties in, and the gardens end up being rubbish tips.'

The agent then asked Vicky if she was a debt collector, to which she replied, 'I suppose I am, in a way,' and hung up. She then went to the local funeral directors that she had seen on her way in and asked the receptionist for information on the recently deceased Mrs Catherine Mitchelson and when the funeral was to take place. The receptionist asked Vicky to wait whilst she went and got one of the directors.

'Did you say "Mrs Catherine Mitchelson"?' asked the director with a frown.

'Yes, that's right. She's my aunt. She recently had a stroke, but sadly died, and I've been waiting to hear when the funeral will be. It's been a while now, and I've heard nothing.'

'I don't know what to say to you, miss. Unless there are two Catherine Mitchelsons in this area, the only Catherine Mitchelson I'm aware of is the one buried in St. Asaph's churchyard, and that funeral took place at least two years ago. This is very unfortunate indeed, and it looks as if someone has been spinning you a yarn.'

It was then that Vicky realised that she had been well and truly conned by her very own cousin and his wife, Mitch and Marnie Mitchelson.

MITCH

If you were to meet Mitch, the impression he gave was that he was perfectly respectable, honest and sincere. In his appearance, his style leaned towards smart-casual rather than trendy. He had dark brown hair which he kept short, a well-trimmed beard, and his chocolate-brown eyes had a permanent twinkle. He was of slim build, with no sign of a paunch, and looked as if he worked out. In fact, he detested exercise and had never belonged to a gym, taken up running, or been a cycling enthusiast. He was certainly good looking, but not in a memorable way, and that was exactly how Mitch wanted it to be.

He had checked out of the bed and breakfast on the Sunday, saying goodbye to Kenneth and the other guests, and moved in with Dorothy Beresford at 10am, as arranged. Dorothy, who usually attended the 10am service at her local church, made an exception this time as she wanted to be accommodating to her new paying guest. Mitch spent the rest of the morning organising his room and was surprised when Dorothy tapped on his door at 12:30 and asked him if he would like something to eat. 'You must be hungry, Daniel. I always have a Sunday roast, and I've got plenty. Would you like some?' Mitch had answered that, if she was sure, then that would be very welcome as he was indeed hungry. Would she mind, though, if he ate it in his room as he still had a lot to do. Dorothy said that was perfectly understandable and would bring a tray along to him. Although Mitch was grateful to Dorothy and taken aback by her kind and generous gesture considering they had only just become acquainted, he didn't want to spend time with her in case she started to ask too many questions. The gesture also revealed to him that his landlady was, at heart, a trusting person who wanted to please. The rest of the day passed by uneventfully, and Mitch had an early night, but not before he rang Marnie to let her know that he had now moved into lodgings.

At 9am on Monday morning, he tapped on Dorothy's kitchen door to say that he wouldn't be needing breakfast as he was off to a meeting. Dressed in a dark blue suit, crisp white shirt, and a multicoloured tie, he had a yellow high-vis jacket over his arm and carried a white hard hat in his hand. With this outfit, he hoped to give the impression that he was a high-powered construction executive off for a site visit. At least, this is what he told Dorothy he was off to do when she had opened her door and exclaimed, 'Well, Daniel, you do look smart. Where are you off to today?'

'Site visit at Shoreham, Dorothy,' he had replied. 'Possible big contract coming up at Shoreham Port, once the Newhaven project comes to an end. Well, I must be off. No time for breakfast, I'm afraid. See you later, and don't do anything I wouldn't do,' he said with a big smile.

'Oh, get away with you,' laughed Dorothy and closed the door.

In actuality, Mitch was off into Brighton. Opening the boot of his car, he threw in the yellow jacket and hat, and drove his car two roads down where he subsequently parked. He then walked down the hill to get the Number 27 bus into Churchill Square, as it was much cheaper to catch a bus than pay the expensive parking charges in Brighton. Once there, he would set about finding an internet café.

He found one near the Clock Tower, where he purchased a large latte, then sat down at a vacant computer and switched it on. Cracking his knuckles, he set to work. *If people think being a con artist* (and Mitch did think of himself as an artist, not just a common or garden con man) *is easy,* he mused, *then they should think again.* He had to juggle all sorts of information, remember names and places, and not get into a muddle with his lies. A memory of his father, Clifford, came to him when he had been caught out in a lie; "remember, son, a liar is worse than a thief". *Well, Dad,* thought Mitch, *I'm a liar and a thief. What would you make of that?* Yep, it wasn't all roses, being a con artist. True, there were some benefits; financial being an obvious one and, when called for, sexual, although he had to admit that sometimes the sex wasn't that enjoyable, but it was a necessary means to an end. The hardest part was coming up with new scenarios. He was also not greedy. This is where a lot of "cons" were going wrong, in his opinion. People were getting too greedy, and the banks were now on red alert when they saw large amounts of money being withdrawn or transferred. So, Mitch kept his demands for money just verging on the reasonable. As for his "personas", he liked to have fun with them and to see what he could get away with. In his experience, there were a lot of very lonely and gullible women out there who would believe anything, and it was this that he played on.

Today, he was searching on a dating website with very specific criteria in mind. It was aimed at people with a certain level of income and Mitch entered a search for women aged between 45 and 60, living in Brighton and the surrounding area. He was looking specifically for a divorcée who was of independent means. A bonus would be if she didn't have dependent children or, better still, no children at all. About an hour later, he had drawn up a list of potential "clients" – he preferred this term to "victim", as it seemed more businesslike – and then whittled the list down further to make it more manageable as there were a lot of women on the site. He finally settled on one to make initial contact with and put the others on the reserve list. She had listed her name as Fiona, and her photograph showed her to be an attractive blond. Although, for Mitch's purposes, looks weren't that important, it made his job a lot easier and pleasant if the women were nice-looking, should he ever meet them face to face.

Hello, I'm Fiona (50), and live in Brighton. Been divorced for a while now and looking for friendship or love (if the right person comes along!) Not into fitness, so please no fitness fanatics. However, living by the seaside, I do enjoy a stroll along the seafront. I also like eating out, going to the cinema and theatre. A fear of flying restricts holidays abroad but am happy to holiday in the UK. I work for a well-known charity as a volunteer. Phew! That's enough about me. What about you?

Mitch liked what he read. A divorced woman on a dating site usually meant two things: she either wanted to play the field and date as many men as possible, or she was looking for a steady relationship which might lead to marriage. In his experience, Mitch had found that some divorced women felt slightly adrift when they were no longer part of a couple, and with that feeling came vulnerability and sometimes a loss of self-esteem. In simple terms, they felt as if they had failed. He didn't know which category Fiona fell into yet, but her profile was straightforward and to the point. Also, he could identify with her on a superficial level in that he, too, wasn't into fitness, and could accommodate strolls along the seafront, where he imagined holding her hand and making her laugh. As to eating out, cinema and theatre, well most of them listed these types of pastimes and, if necessary, he could be accommodating. Fear of flying, though, was a bonus. She wouldn't be expecting him to whisk her off on a romantic getaway-break abroad where he was expected to pay for everything. A weekend away in the English countryside could be provided if it was absolutely essential, as long as it was a "two for one" deal. He took note that she worked as a volunteer, which probably meant that she was financially stable. As to where she lived, he would find out soon enough, so he sent her a "wink" and a "wave" and logged off. He then went onto a larger, and more generalised, site, which was less select and, in Mitch's opinion, a bit like a cattle market. Furthermore, the financial rewards would probably be less but at least it would keep the "coffers" topped up.

*

A few weeks ago, when Mitch had first searched the site, he had come across someone calling herself "Nurse Susie", aged 40. She lived in Guildford and worked as an agency nurse for both a private hospital and the local NHS hospital. Her list of interests was nothing out of the ordinary, but what caught his eye was the revelation that, due to the nature of her job, she was often too tired to socialise much. She had further said that she was looking for someone "to make me laugh and take me out of myself".

Analysing "Nurse Susie's" posting, Mitch read into it that she was probably lonely and her life outside of work a bit mundane. This gave him an idea as to how to reel her in. The thing about Mitch was that he was thorough in his research. He wasn't a lazy or sloppy con artist. He approached all of his "projects" professionally and methodically, and his elaborate scams were carefully thought-out and painstakingly plotted.

Susie had listed Guildford as her location, and she had also said that going to the theatre was something she liked doing. However, she had contradicted herself when she had revealed that she didn't have much energy for going out. This told Mitch that Susie probably didn't go to the theatre or cinema that often, and, in all likelihood, watched a lot of television. Searching for information about Guildford, he read that it had its own theatre, which was considered to be an important venue in that it often put on plays that were eventually destined for the West End. So, Mitch had found out what current play was being performed and looked to see who the cast were. Because there was only a handful of actors in the play, their names were listed with a brief mention of their acting roles to date. One of the cast members, who was playing the part of the butler, was a minor actor who had appeared in British soaps, usually in non-speaking parts, but who would be recognisable to anyone who watched such programmes. So, he had downloaded a photograph of the actor and then uploaded it onto the dating website and set up a profile using the actor's name. Mitch then contacted Susie, posing as the actor who was called Tim, instinctively knowing that she would be grateful for any response, as her photograph depicted a plain-looking woman with a nervous smile. Also, he guessed that she would be thrilled and excited by the prospect of being in contact with someone who had been on the television, and it would probably not occur to her to initially question why someone like that would contact her.

'*Hello, Nurse Susie,*' Mitch (posing as Tim) had typed. '*I'm Tim and I notice you list the theatre as one of your interests. I'm an actor.*'

She had answered almost immediately. '*Hello, Tim. Yes, I do like the theatre when I get a chance to go. I thought your face looked familiar. I must have seen you on the TV, I think.*'

'*That's right, Susie. I've been in a number of things.*'

'*What have you been in?*'

'*Ooh, now let me think...* Eastenders, Holby City, Emmerdale, Corrie – *you know, all the nation's favourite soaps.*'

And Susie was immediately hooked. It was that easy.

Today, when Mitch had logged on, he saw a message from Susie was waiting.

'*Hi, Tim. How are you? Haven't heard from you lately. Is all okay?*'

'*Hello, Susie! Huge apologies. I don't know if you're aware of this, but I'm in a play at the moment in your local theatre. So, what with rehearsals, etc., it's all been a bit busy.*'

Within a short space of time, a reply came back.

'*That's okay, Tim. It must be exciting being an actor. I didn't know you were here in Guildford. I must admit, I haven't seen the play. Sorry.*'

Mitch had replied, '*Don't be sorry. Hey, I've got an idea. How about I send you a ticket so that you can come and see me in the play, and we could meet up afterwards for a drink?*'

'*Really! That would be wonderful. How exciting. But you don't know where I live.*'

'*Well, Susie, I could leave a ticket at the box office for you or, if you're happy to put your address in an email to me, I'll put one in the post for you. Are you free next week in the evening, or are you working nights?*'

'I don't work a night shift so any night would be great. This is so kind of you, Tim, and I can't wait to meet you. If you can give me your email address, I'll give you mine.'

It really is this easy, thought Mitch. *Not only have I almost got her off the site now and into the private domain, but I'll soon have her home address.* He then set up a fictitious email account, logged back onto the dating site and sent Susie the email address.

Deciding he had done enough work for now, he closed down the computer and headed out of the café and decided to do some shopping. His first stop was the large Boots near the Clock Tower, where he purchased face tan, hair dye and a black headband. He then went into a discount store, where he bought a plain white sheet in the homeware department. Deciding to explore a bit more, he wandered around until he came to a maze of lanes, which he discovered was known as The Lanes, and then headed for the seafront where he imagined he was a tourist and had fish and chips on the pier. Not wanting to head further up into Hove, as he was without his car, he caught a bus back to his lodgings in Saltdean. Letting himself in with the spare key Dorothy had given him, he could hear the television on in the living room and decided not to disturb her, as she would probably ask him about his day, and he would be forced to tell more lies. He had spent all morning telling lies, and he didn't feel like telling any more for now.

After taking a shower, Mitch fell asleep for a few hours. Waking refreshed and keen to start on his evening tasks, he crept along the hallway and quietly opened the front door. He then walked two streets down to get his car and drove to a pub he had seen earlier and hoped that they had free Wi-Fi. He was in luck. Also, it wasn't very busy as it was still early evening, so he bought himself a beer, found a table in the corner and switched on his laptop. Using the pub's Wi-Fi connection, he connected to the internet and went to his new email account where he found a message from Susie, and set about replying to her.

From: <TimStar1>
To: <NurseSusie12>
SUBJECT: Ticket on its way!

Hi, Susie! As promised, the complimentary ticket will wing its way to you as soon as you give me your address. Can't wait to meet you face to face. Ciao! Tim xx

Mitch pressed "Send" and waited for a reply, taking a long slurp of his beer. A "pinging" sound from his laptop signalled the arrival of an email, and he laughed as he realised she must be glued to her computer just waiting to hear from him. He was right. It was an email from Susie giving him her home address so that he could forward the ticket.

Mitch disconnected from his email account and went on to one of the property information sites he used. First, he typed in Susie's postcode to see if there were any properties for sale in that area, and what the sale price was. Nothing came up for sale and so he went on to another property website and typed in the postcode to search for the history of "sold" properties. Here, he had more luck and was able to see how much a similar property to Susie's would cost to buy. He was pleasantly surprised because, although he knew that nurses generally were not that well-paid, he reasoned that Susie must earn sufficient money to be able to have afforded to buy her house, which was described on the property website as a two-bed terraced property in a gated mews development.

The reason he carried out such research was to gauge an idea of her financial situation. If, for example, she lived in a one-bedroom flat in a built-up area of Guildford, or was a tenant, then he would not proceed because the financial gains would not be worth the time and effort. Further searches revealed that the property had never been listed for rent, and so he continued with his "Nurse Susie" project.

The next thing he did was to log on to the theatre's website and go to the "booking" section. There was only one price for tickets, and he was gratified to see that they weren't too expensive. An online seating plan also enabled him to choose a seat the furthest away from the stage. Having ordered and paid for the ticket, and put in Nurse Susie's address for delivery, he then logged onto the dating website where he had found Fiona and signed in as "Dan". She had waved back at him, and added a smiley face, so this gave him encouragement.

'Hello, Fiona. Thanks for returning my wave and adding a smile! I like your photo. Did you have it retouched?' Mitch knew he was taking a chance with this cheeky comment. She would either find it amusing and take part in the banter, or she would be offended and not reply. Taking no chances, however, he quickly added, *'Only joking. You look lovely.'*

Almost immediately a reply came back. *'Cheeky! No, it's all natural. I even have my own teeth and hair – ha ha.'*

'Phew, that's a relief!' Mitch knew he was on to a winner. *'I notice your location is Brighton. I'm working in Shoreham next week. Fancy meeting up for lunch?'*

'Yes, I'd like that. Do you know Brighton very well?'

'Not that well. I know the seafront and that's about it.'

'Well, there's a nice beachfront café to the right of the pier, and there's parking along the seafront. Is Thursday any good?'

'Yep, suits me fine. Shall we say 12:30? And we can keep chatting online in the meantime.'

Having achieved what he set out to do, Mitch signed off and finished his beer.

Arriving back at his lodgings, he let himself in. Dorothy's light was still on in the living room, so Mitch shouted through the door, 'Night night, Dorothy. See you in the morning,' and went to his room.

God, he thought, *it's hard work and very tiring being a con artist*, and he immediately fell into a deep sleep.

MARNIE

Marnie was getting bored. Cooped up in a tiny one-bedroom flat in the backstreets of Luton, with no one to talk to, and minimal contact from Mitch, she found comfort in eating and drinking – usually, shop-bought meat pies and ready-mixed gin and tonic in a can. She had a particular fondness for the pink gin and tonic variety, which was very sweet. As a result, not only was she piling on more weight, but she was beginning to drink at lunchtime as well, which was not good. Still, Mitch was coming back this weekend and so she had something to look forward to. She knew he may not talk to her very much, because he was always so focussed on his work, but at least he would be company for her.

SUSIE

As promised, the ticket for Tim's play arrived for the Wednesday evening. Susie took extra care with her appearance, changing her outfit many times before settling on a mid-length floral dress and shoes with kitten heels. As she wore flat shoes at work, she felt good putting on shoes with heels, which added a couple of inches to her height and made her legs appear slimmer. She had gone to the hairdressers for a trim and felt that she looked presentable. Make-up was not really her thing, having never learnt how to put it on properly, so she dabbed powder on her face to take off the shine, a bit of pale pink blusher, a coating of mascara and pale pink lipstick. She knew she wasn't a stunner and had a momentary feeling of anxiety as to why Tim had chosen her. But he had, and she swept the worry aside.

The theatre was within walking distance, and she arrived to find a throng of people in the foyer. This pleased her, because it meant the play was doing well. People began to make their way to their seats, and Susie was a bit dismayed to find that her seat was right at the back of the theatre, which meant that she wouldn't be able to make eye contact with Tim. She had imagined he would be seeking her out, and their eyes would meet and a subtle acknowledgment between them would occur. Sighing, she sat down and reminded herself she would be seeing him afterwards.

The lights dimmed, and the play began. Twenty minutes into the play, Tim hadn't yet appeared. Most of the action was taking place in the drawing room of a stately home, in which a group of people were sat around talking. The leading lady rang a bell on the table, and a door was opened. 'You rang, m'lady,' said the butler on entering the room. Susie gasped, because this was Tim. Here he was, on stage! She looked at the people sitting either side of her, because she wanted to tell them that he was her boyfriend. She felt so proud and sat up straighter. The leading lady asked the butler to remove the tea tray, which he did with a bow and left the room. Susie was disappointed further, because Tim didn't appear again, and he was the only reason she was there. She had also assumed that he would have had a much bigger speaking part and felt slightly deflated.

The play ended and everyone filed out. Susie wasn't sure what to do, and so she waited in the foyer until it was virtually empty. It occurred to her that perhaps the actors only came out once the foyer and auditorium were clear. When she realised that she was the only person left in the foyer, she found a member of staff and asked where the actors were because she was supposed to meet one of them. The response she got was that all the actors had left immediately after the play had finished. Susie asked if she knew where they had gone. 'Do they go to a particular pub for a drink, or a restaurant, perhaps?'

'I'm sorry,' the member of staff replied, 'I think they all go their separate ways. I'm sorry I can't be of more help.'

Susie was experiencing a mixture of disappointment and bewilderment. She reasoned that there must have been a good reason why he hadn't come out to meet her, because he had gone to the trouble of sending her a ticket and he wouldn't have done that if he wasn't serious about meeting up. Rationalising the situation in this way, Susie began to feel better and, although it was late, she decided to email Tim when she arrived home.

From: <NurseSusie12>
To: <TimStar1>
SUBJECT: This Evening

Hi, Tim – I came to the play this evening and saw you briefly onstage. I would have given you a little wave, but I was sat right at the back. I thought we were going to meet up afterwards and was disappointed when we didn't. I was so looking forward to it. What happened? Susie

Susie wasn't expecting a reply, so she logged out of her email address and got ready for bed. After the initial nervous excitement at the start of the evening, she now felt mildly depressed.

The next morning, she felt too downhearted to do her shift at the private hospital. She hated letting her fellow nurses down, but this time she put herself first for once. Also, she wanted to see if Tim had replied to her email, and she couldn't do that if she was at work. Logging on to her emails, she saw that Tim had indeed sent a reply.

From: <TimStar1>
To: <NurseSusie12>
SUBJECT: This Evening

Susie, Sweetie! I am soo sorry. Can you forgive me? There was an aftershow party which I <u>simply</u> had to attend because the director and producer had organised it. Also, it looks as if the play is going to the West End, so it was très important that I show my face. I was disappointed too, my *sweet. I wanted to give you a "mwah mwah" on both cheeks and introduce you to my fellow thespians. Susie, dearest, this acting business is cutthroat and so many people want to stab you in the back. It's a dog-eat-dog world, and you're only as good as your next role. I hope you understand, then, why I couldn't meet you afterwards. Acting comes before anything else – sadly.*

Love Tim X

Mitch felt he'd struck just the right note of explanation and conciliation and was proved right when Susie replied that she understood perfectly and expressed excitement at the news of the play going to the West End.

'Would you like to see the play when it goes to the West End?' Mitch had asked. 'I can get you a ticket. Just say the word, Susie!'

And Susie replied, 'Yes please, Tim.'

Mitch's plan was shaping up very nicely.

MITCH

As Mitch was always telling Marnie, you had to speculate to accumulate and that involved taking risks. He was also always reminding her that in order to "win some you had to lose some", and he'd experienced a few losses in his time when some of his "projects" – as he liked to call them – had not progressed as planned and had to be abandoned. The problem was that there were simply too many con men out their now, and they were getting better and better at their craft. Take those, for example, who pretended they were serving in Afghanistan or Syria, or were servicemen who had fought for their country and were invalided out. And, of course, the con men who worked in teams who, it appeared, had conning down to a fine art and managed to get thousands of pounds out of women who they never even met. Mitch was amazed at how gullible these women were, but then there was an abundance of lonely and vulnerable women who believed any old bit of flannel. Some, however, were not daft; keen, perhaps, but not daft. Take Bev, for instance, who had been one of Mitch's failed projects.

Bev had been on holiday to Turkey a few times and found herself on the receiving end of attention from some of the young waiters in the resort of Bodrum where she always stayed. As an older woman, she was becoming invisible to men in her own country. In Turkey, however, being mature, curvaceous, and having long dark hair and olive skin, gave her an advantage. She had been flattered and pursued by them, and even agreed to having sex with two of them. *Well, who wouldn't?* she asked herself.

A woman in her late forties being pursued by younger men, with their dark, brooding looks, and being clearly enamoured of her, would be mad to turn down a bit of Turkish Delight. However, Bev wanted money and the waiters expected her to buy things for them – not the other way round.

So, after her last holiday to Turkey, she decided that she needed to meet a wealthy man and subsequently cast her net internationally, but with a preference for "Mediterranean" men and uploaded a photograph of herself in a belly dancing costume. She was aware of some of the pitfalls of internet dating and countries to avoid, but still held a romantic notion of finding her ideal mate. Thus, when Asil Cemil Burakgazi – a restaurant owner from Bodrum – contacted her, she let all her defences down very quickly. Yes, she did know Bodrum, she replied. *I've holidayed there a number of times.'* Yes, she had eaten in many restaurants. No, she didn't know that he owned most of the restaurants in Bodrum. And she had queried this with a, *'Why would I?'*

'Well, my gorgeous curvy English lady,' he had replied, *'I am well-known in Bodrum because of my restaurants which always get good reviews.'*

Bev, who rarely took anyone at face value and certainly didn't always believe what people said, decided to test him. She had eaten at a restaurant in Bodrum Marina a few times, and the owner – who was bald, short, plump, and had no facial hair – looked nothing like the man in the photograph on the dating website. Thus, in response to Asil Cemil Burakgazi's claim that he owned many restaurants, she had mentioned the restaurant. If he replied that it was one of his, then she would know he was lying because his photograph showed him to be a handsome man with a full head of dark brown hair and a neatly trimmed beard.

Mitch was a very thorough con artist and had anticipated questions of this sort. Hence, he had carried out his usual due diligence on all the social media sites and could reply to Bev's question with some confidence. *'Sadly not, my beautiful Bev,'* he had replied. *'That one is owned by my cousin. Most of mine are in Bodrum City. Perhaps you ate at one of them?'*

Bev, who had no way of knowing whether or not he was telling the truth, decided, on this occasion, to give him the benefit of the doubt.

'So, Bev, what do you say? Are you interested in me? I think you will agree that I am not looking bad, but perhaps I am coming across – as you English say – a bit large-headed.'

Bev had replied that he meant "not bad-looking" and "big-headed", but agreed that he was handsome and added a smiley emoji after her text.

'Yes, that is what I meant, beautiful lady. I am looking for someone who is my other half. I think we would fit very well together, like two beans in a pod.'

'You mean two peas in a pod, I think,' replied Bev and added two laughing emojis after her text.

'Your English language is so difficult. You have many funny sayings, but that is part of your charm, I think. Let me tell you something about myself. My name, Asil Cemil, means "nobleman" and "kind-hearted". My surname means "warrior". So, beautiful English lady, I am a kind-hearted nobleman with a fighting spirit. I would be all man to you, if you know what I mean.'

Bev had found herself getting hot and flushed in the face. *My God*, she thought, *he's the man of my dreams.* Rich and virile – just what I need – and so she was swept away on a tide of excitement and lust.

Over the next few days, matters proceeded quickly. He told her that he was coming to London soon to open another Turkish restaurant in the Stoke Newington area with his brothers, who lived in London. They owned many restaurants in that area, and he was overseeing the new project as well as investing money into the business. This would mean he would be spending a lot of time in London and they could get to know each other better and have some romantic evenings together. *'Perhaps,'* he had suggested, *'you would like to sample my special kebab? It is extra-large'.* At writing this, Mitch had burst out laughing at his rude innuendo, and took a moment to compose himself. It was moments like this that made his job – and he did view it as a job – worthwhile.

A few days later, he went in for the kill. Telling Bev that he was booking his plane ticket to travel to London in two days' time, he asked if she would be "amenable" to transferring £5000 to the Western Union branch in Crawley, which was near Gatwick Airport. He was sorry to ask this of her, he had added, but the exchange rate was so poor in Turkey at the moment that he wanted to get as much sterling as possible to ensure he had sufficient funds for the trip. *'I want to spoil you, beautiful Bev,'* he had said. *'Wine and dine you, and perhaps you will repay me by wearing that very sexy belly dancer's costume you wore in your photograph. I am a hot-blooded Turk, Bev. Are you ready for me?'*

Putting any subconscious concerns to the back of her mind, she had trustingly, and somewhat excitedly, agreed and then the silly cow – as Mitch subsequently thought of her - had gone and spoilt it. Not only did she not transfer the money, but she had taken it upon herself to go up to London with an envelope full of cash and introduce herself to his brothers. She had found the road with the Turkish restaurants and had enquired in every one of them if they knew a Turkish restaurant owner called Asil Cemil Burakgazi from Bodrum. Not one of them had ever heard of him, and Bev realised that she had almost been the victim of a con man.

On returning home, she had contacted her fake Turkish restaurant owner and relayed all of this to him, and then deleted her account for the time being. She felt she'd had a lucky escape, but it brought home to her how easily she had been drawn into the scam. It then dawned on her as to how this person, whoever he was, and she doubted that he was even Turkish, had known about her holidays in Bodrum. There could be only one explanation – her social media posts. Not wanting to disappear from social media altogether, she switched her profiles from "public" to "private", so that only her family and close friends had access to her life.

For his part, Mitch put it down to experience and set about finding a new target; a female with less initiative and forwardness.

FIONA

Having given Dan directions for their lunch date, Fiona sat and waited. It was a sunny day, with a slight breeze, and the sea sparkled as if there were millions of diamonds dancing on the surface. Office workers sat in groups, chatting and laughing, mothers with their young children eating ice lollies walked by, and elderly couples strolled arm in arm. Noisy foreign exchange students sat on the pebbly beach playing their music loudly and shrieking excitedly. If she had looked up towards the railings on Brighton Pier, she would have seen a man watching her.

Having got there early and found a parking space, Mitch walked onto the pier and kept his eyes on the outdoor café where they were meeting. He saw her as soon as she came into view. She was wearing a dress that fitted her perfectly, in soft colours of turquoise, peach and pale green. He noticed that her shoes and handbag were a matching cream colour, and that her blond hair was styled in a neat bob. Rather alarmingly, she reminded Mitch of his cousin, Vicky. First impressions were that she was very feminine and very attractive; more importantly, she looked to be well-heeled. Everything about her exuded class, taste, and money. He exited the pier and made his way down the steps to the café.

Having only seen a slightly blurred photograph of "Dan", Fiona was surprised when a good-looking man came up to her and asked if the seat at the table was free. It didn't register with her immediately, and then the penny dropped. 'You're Dan,' she said with a smile.

'Yep, that's me, and you must be Fiona,' he replied, sitting down opposite her.

For their date, he had chosen to wear a blue and white check shirt, which was open at the neck, and a royal blue, rather than navy blue, suit as Mitch wanted to give the impression of a successful company director who could wear what he wanted to the office, rather than the generic navy suit with white shirt worn by middle management employees. Close up, Fiona noticed that his dark brown hair had flecks of grey at the temple and that his neatly trimmed beard, which she found very attractive, also had a sprinkling of grey.

For his part, Mitch noticed that, although Fiona wore make-up, it was subtly applied so as to appear natural. Also, he was very relieved to see that her blond hair had no roots showing, which meant she was either a natural blond or took real pride in her appearance. He couldn't abide those women who dyed their hair blond and then let the dark roots show through. He thought it looked awful and, if he was honest, a bit common. Everything about Fiona was classy and tasteful. 'You look lovely, if I may say so,' remarked Mitch who, for once, was speaking the truth.

'And you don't look bad yourself,' Fiona replied with a grin, revealing perfectly straight, white teeth.

'Right, that's the introductions over with,' said Mitch, rubbing the palms of his hands together. 'What can I get you to drink? And do you want to eat, because I'm starving?'

'A glass of Sauvignon Blanc, please, and can I suggest the chicken salad wrap with sweet potato fries. It's very good here.'

'Okey doke. Won't be long.'

As Mitch walked away, Fiona looked at his slim build and the upright way he carried himself. He obviously looked after himself, which impressed her. His brown eyes, slightly tanned face, neatly trimmed beard and short hair, all made for a favourable impression on her. She found him attractive and could already imagine herself getting up close with him. *Oops,* she thought, *I'm getting a bit ahead of myself here.*

Lunch went extremely well. They discovered that they had quite a few things in common during their formative years. Both had left school at 15 and worked in fairly boring jobs. Then, they had both returned to education at age 18; he to study for an HND in management studies, which eventually led to his current job as an operations director for a company overseeing and maintaining British seaports, and she to study for a Certificate in Secretarial Studies and Office Management, which is how she had met her husband when he employed her as his office manager. Both were divorced. His not amicably, and hers so-so but with no real hard feelings. As to the question of children, Fiona told Dan that they had never got round to having any. Dan, however, revealed that he had a son, aged 13, who lived with his ex-wife. He told Fiona that he saw him as much as possible, but that his "ex" made things very difficult. 'Anyway,' he had said, 'let's not go down that road.' He lifted up his glass of wine, saying, 'Here's to us.'

He had offered to buy lunch, but Fiona insisted on going halves. He then announced that, regrettably, he had to get back to work and wished he could have spent many more hours with her as he had enjoyed her company very much. 'Would you,' he had asked, 'like to have dinner with me next week?'

'Yes please! That would be great,' replied Fiona, and she had given him her mobile number.

Mitch felt jubilant after lunch. Not only had he spent a couple of hours in the company of an attractive and a genuinely nice person, but he could tell that she liked him. *I haven't lost my kerb appeal yet,* he thought. Walking to his car, he put more money into the meter and headed to the internet café near the station. Now he had to speed things up with Susie, as the money he had conned his cousin out of was dwindling, and Marnie was beginning to moan. Logging onto his fake email address, he contacted Susie.

From: <TimStar1>
To: <NurseSusie12>
Subject: Bad news and good news!

Dearest Susie – I have some bad news. The producer has decided not to take the play to the West End and so it will not be possible to organise our meet-up in London. I soo wanted you to see me in a West End production, and then I could have taken you backstage to meet everyone. But that's showbiz, dearest Susie. Full of ups and downs. All is not lost though – I have some good news! An American agent came to the theatre the other night and was very impressed with my performance. He felt I had such a strong stage presence, that – wait for it – he wants me to fly out to Los Angeles to do a screen test!!! CAN YOU BELIEVE IT?! Moi – a Hollywood actor. Perhaps, after all, I will be your Hollywood heart-throb. How exciting is that, my lovely Susie. Must dash, the phone is ringing. It might be my agent! Love Tim xoxo

Although Susie found her job as a nurse rewarding and, in the main, very satisfying, on occasion – such as today's shift – all it seemed to consist of was emptying bedpans, changing bandages, dressing wounds, and listening to all kinds of moans and groans. So, pouring herself a large cup of coffee, she logged onto her email address, and found Tim's email to her. Ignoring the fact that, once again, she had still not met Tim, who seemed to be very adept at not keeping his promises, she found herself transported out of her very ordinary existence to a world of glamour and began to fantasise about living in Hollywood with him and going to premiers dressed in designer clothes, and spending her days in beauty salons, or sitting by their private pool drinking cocktails.

From: <NurseSusie12>
To: <TimStar1>
Subject: Bad news and good news!

Dearest Tim – or should I call you Brad? Ha ha. That is wonderful news. I am so pleased for you. I have had such an awful day, but your email has completely lifted my spirits. Let me know when you leave for LA. If I can, I will come and see you off at the airport. Lots of love, Susie (your biggest fan!) xoxo

MITCH

In the end, it all came down to good planning. It was like doing a jigsaw puzzle, Mitch thought. Get all the outside edges in place first like a frame, then put the other pieces in clusters of colours as the picture on the box depicted until finally all the pieces slotted into the right place and created a complete picture. Mitch also had a carefully planned routine. From Monday to Friday, he would stay with Mrs B (as he had now begun to affectionately call her) and every morning, after breakfast, he would bid her adieu and go to work. Sometimes she asked where he was off to, just out of general politeness, and he always gave the same answer – he was either off to Shoreham or Newhaven. She had no reason to disbelieve him, which suited him well. Early on a Saturday morning, or sometimes late on a Friday evening, he would travel up to Luton to spend the weekend with Marnie, returning late on a Sunday evening.

Today, for example, Dorothy came out into the hallway and wished him a good day. 'Off to Shoreham is it today, or Newhaven?' she asked.

'You know me, Mrs B; a creature of habit – sunny Shoreham today. See you later,' he had replied.

In actuality, Mitch was off exploring. He had exhausted the Brighton area and gone as far as the outskirts of Worthing, travelling through Shoreham and Lancing on the way. This morning, he was headed in the opposite direction. From his lodgings in Saltdean, he drove through Peacehaven and round the one-way system in

Newhaven, and then followed a long road until he came to a large roundabout where Eastbourne was signposted to the right. On the spur of the moment, he turned left until he came to another roundabout and took a right turn to Lewes. Passing through the Cuilfail Tunnel, and not having a clue where he was, he turned left and then right at a small roundabout and left again, which took him into a large Tesco supermarket carpark. Exiting the car, he walked through a pedestrian cut-through and found himself on a pathway by the river, which led into the town of Lewes.

He found Lewes charming; just like a traditional town should be. Independent shops lined either side of the road, mixed in with such staples as Waterstones, Boots and Costa Coffee. There were quite a few jewellery shops, and he came across one by chance that had originally designed jewellery in the window and was reasonably priced. Mitch never wasted money, but sometimes investments had to be made to ensure success in the future. He went in and purchased some silver earrings with green tassels, which the attractive girl behind the counter assured him were very "on trend" at the moment. She also asked him if they were a gift, because she would gift wrap them for him. Mitch replied that they were for his girlfriend, to which the girl replied, with a smile, 'Lucky girlfriend.'

Making his way back to the car, he drove back through the tunnel and turned left and headed towards Eastbourne. He passed a signpost for Glyndebourne which he knew was a place where posh people went to hear opera. Further along, he saw a sign for Charleston Farmhouse which was open to the public and had a tearoom. He made a note to go online and investigate further, as he didn't have time to explore the farmhouse today. From then on, it was more or less a straight road into Eastbourne. However, once there, and unfamiliar with the roads and traffic system, he decided to park near the seafront and stop for lunch. He found it easier to park in Eastbourne and not as expensive as Brighton. It was also less crowded, and altogether much less frantic.

He headed towards the pier, which had recently been renovated after a fire, and treated himself to fish and chips. For a brief moment, he felt as if he was on holiday. However, this was all for research and everything had to be noted down for future reference. Nothing could be left to chance. Heading back to his car, he drove out of Eastbourne, but took a wrong turn and found himself on the back road. He passed a sign for Beachy Head, and eventually came to Cuckmere Haven with its winding ribbon-like river flowing through a landscape he had never seen the likes of before. *Wow!* he thought. Passing by a country park and lovely flint cottages, the scenery was far removed from the industrial steel town he and Marnie had come from and had lived in for many years. He wished she was here to share this experience instead of being stuck in the one-bedroom flat in Luton.

EDITH

Edith, now in her early 70s and never married, reflected on how life seemed to have passed her by. Having devoted her working life to teaching, rising to the position of headmistress at an all-girls school on the outskirts of Brighton, and caring for her elderly mother to whom she had been devoted until she had passed away, Edith realised that she had never really done anything for herself. She couldn't even say that she had ever had a proper boyfriend, let alone any marriage proposals. Her mother had dominated her, and it became clear to Edith that no boy or man would ever be good enough. Edith suspected, and did feel a touch of guilt at such an uncharitable thought, that this was her mother's way of keeping Edith just where she needed her to be – at home, looking after her every need.

Now, with her mother no longer alive and her teaching career behind her, Edith suddenly had time on her hands, and plenty of it. She had also realised that she had been surrounded by women for most of her life: her grandmother and mother, and then the girls at school. *What I want,* she thought, *is a male companion.* Someone to go to the theatre with, or the opera, or art exhibitions. Someone cultured. Perhaps even someone to go on holiday with, as long as it was in the United Kingdom as she didn't have a passport. In any event, going abroad held little interest for her, as she wanted to see more of her own country. What she didn't want, and she shuddered at the thought and immediately felt embarrassed, was someone who wanted sexual intercourse. The very idea of it alarmed her because she was still a virgin and felt horrified at what having intercourse might entail. Growing up, the school she went to didn't teach about procreation or precaution, and her mother never spoke about such things. Being the headmistress of an all-girls school did, of course, cover such matters, but Edith delegated that responsibility to the biology teacher. The big question now, was how could she meet such a companion?

The answer presented itself a few days later. Once a week, she met up with a group of retired women teachers who lived in the area. Having settled themselves down at their favourite café in Rottingdean, Edith suddenly announced, to the surprise of the group, that she wanted a man.

'I want a male companion,' she exclaimed.

'Don't we all, Edith,' Glenys replied.

'I don't want one. They're nothing but trouble. I'm quite happy with my Bobo. Aren't I, Bobo?' And here Miriam patted her dog, Bobo, on the head, who obligingly barked a "woof" in response.

'What I mean,' explained Edith, 'is that I would like some male company. That's all. But I don't know how to go about getting some.'

'You could try internet dating,' responded Glenys. 'I've been doing it for a while. I haven't met anyone yet I really like, but I've been on some nice dates and, to be honest, some not so nice ones. If you don't like the person, you don't have to see them again.'

'You kept that very quiet, Glenys Dennison. Why so secretive?' chipped in another member of the group.

'I wasn't being secretive, Margaret. It's a personal thing, isn't it? But seeing as Edith has raised the subject, I'm suggesting it to her.'

'So, Edith, I'm going to write down the two sites I use. It's very easy. You upload a photograph of yourself online, and then you complete a profile which gives all the basic information about yourself; your likes and dislikes, for example. You don't need to go into too much detail but try to find something interesting about yourself so that potential suitors will want to know a bit more about you.'

'You have to be very careful,' added Margaret. 'There's a lot of con men on these sites, and weirdos. I've seen programmes about it on the TV.'

'That's why,' said Glenys in response to Margaret's comment, but looking at Edith, 'don't, under any circumstances, reveal too much personal and private information such as financial details or your address. And only conduct your messaging through the site, until such time as you feel it's safe or appropriate to message offline and you've exchanged telephone numbers. Better still, not until you've actually met the person face to face a few times. Now, Edith, if you have any problems with getting your profile done, just call me. Now, I must dash. I've got a date later.'

Edith had never felt so much excitement or trepidation in her life. Saying farewell to her friends, she rushed home, keen to get on with her profile.

SUSIE

Susie was getting worried. She hadn't heard from Tim for a few days and wasn't sure whether to make contact as she didn't want to be seen to be too eager. She had gone online a few times to see if he was still on the site and was reassured when she saw that he was always "offline". She had also got into the habit of obsessively "googling" him to see if there was any news in the media about his trip to Los Angeles, or any reviews about his part in the play. Apart from a few cursory lines on Wikipedia about which acting school he had gone to, and his career to-date, there was very little other information, and he didn't even exist on IMDb. She did find a brief reference to the play in the local Guildford newspaper, but as he had only a supporting role, his name wasn't mentioned. Still, she reminded herself that she had seen him on the television a few times, usually walk-on parts in BBC dramas, and in one particular long-running advertisement for engine oil which had ended a while ago, so he was a real actor. The opportunity of going to Los Angeles, therefore, would be the big break that would launch his career stateside. He was getting on a bit, though, she thought, and was already beginning to get worried for him and how she would comfort him in his disappointment should nothing come of his screen test.

Logging on to her email account, she sent him a message asking how he was and if he had any news regarding his trip to America. Almost immediately, a reply came back. *He must have been waiting for an email from me,* she thought to herself, and was simultaneously comforted and reassured by this.

From: <TimStar1>
To: <NurseSusie12>
Subject: How are you?

My dearest darling Susie – I am so sorry I haven't been in touch. In answer to your question – "How are you?" – I'm afraid to say that I'm in a trough of despondency, which is why I haven't been in contact. It looks as if my one and only chance of being a Hollywood "A-lister" – because, let's face it, Susie, old gal, I ain't no spring chicken – is scuppered before I even get there. The problem is money. Even though I, personally, get rave reviews for my performances, an actor treads the boards for love, not money. Remember dear old Chatterton, the unappreciated poet who died of poverty alone in his attic! And he was only 17!!

Susie, who thought 17 wasn't very old and didn't even know who Chatterton was, was mindful not to appear ignorant or uncultured.

From: <NurseSusie12>
To: <TimStar1>
Subject: How are you?

Dearest Tim – yes, indeed, poor old Chatterton. I wouldn't wish that on anyone! What do you need the money for, though, Tim? Susie x

From: <TimStar1>
To: <NurseSusie12>
Subject: How are you?

Well, it's like this, Susie, my sweet. I have to pay for my return flight to LA, and the accommodation – one has to stay in the right hotel where you can see and be seen – and I need some new clothes. I'm ashamed to say that some of mine have holes in them! It's all about appearance and presentation over there. I just don't have £15,000, which is what I would need. Yours – a very downhearted Tim

From: <NurseSusie12>
To: <TimStar1>
Subject: How are you?

Darling Tim – £15,000! That's an awful lot of money!!

From: <TimStar1>
To: <NurseSusie12>
Subject: How are you?

Susie My Sweet – That's nothing in the overall scheme of things. Some actors pay that for one night in a Bel Air or Beverly Hills hotel. I've chosen the Hotel Angeleno near the Getty Museum, on the outskirts of downtown LA. A lot of well-known actors and directors go there to discuss projects in peace and privacy. Even though it is a reasonably priced hotel, I will probably have to stay in a suite in order to convey the right impression to visiting directors and producers, and also pay for any entertaining, so I have budgeted for £5,000. This acting business is all about appearances, and networking – knowing the right people. I sometimes feel I'm selling my soul!! Oh, why is life so difficult!? You know, Susie, I've never told you this – and I feel I can reveal more to you now that we are getting closer – but I have not had it easy. Virtually starving when I first started out, and I had to do all sorts of dreadful things to earn a meagre crust. Sometimes when I think about it, I hang my head in shame. I do hope I've not put you off me, Susie. I don't think I could bear it. You're my rock at the moment. Love Tim X

Susie had read nothing about this difficult part of his career on Wikipedia. Scant though the information was, she had read that he came from a supportive family, had gone to a good school, and had trained at a well-known London acting school. So, she was a bit puzzled by what he had said. However, he had signed off "Love Tim" with a large "kiss". He had never used the word "love" before in his previous emails, and this caused her heart to flutter. She spent the next few minutes indulging in one of her fantasies where she and Tim had got married and had a centre-page spread in one of the celebrity magazines.

A pinging sound on her computer brought her out of her reverie. It was an email from Tim.

From: <TimStar1>
To: NurseSusie12>
Subject: How are you?

Are you there, Susie? You've gone quiet on me. Have I blown it with you? You've probably looked me up on Wikipedia. Let's just say Susie, not everything goes out in the public domain. For the sake of my parents and siblings, there are some things they don't need to know – if you get my drift? Tim x

Susie felt guilty, and replied "Yes, I'm sorry, I did look you up but only because I couldn't quite believe that someone famous would be interested in me".

"Susie, Susie, Susie," came the reply, "I haven't forgotten where I've come from. I meet a lot of insincere people in this business and, you probably won't be surprised to hear this, I get targeted by young female ingénues who promise me all sorts of delights if I can help them climb the ladder to success. But, Susie, I'm not interested in them. Even though we haven't yet met, I only have eyes for you because you come across as a sincere, warm and honest human being. I'm beginning to have strong feelings of love for you. You've also raised me out of my trough of depression just talking with you like this. You are very special to me". And he had signed off with two large "kisses".

From: <NurseSusie12>
To: <TimStar1>
Subject: How are you?

I'm glad I've been of help to you, Tim, and you are very special to me too. Could I ask, though, what the other £10,000 is for?

Susie xx

Mitch was taken aback by the curtness of Susie's response and the coolness of the tone that had crept in. Sensing a possible withdrawing on her part, and the possibility that she was becoming suspicious, Mitch decided that decisive action was needed.

From: <TimStar1>
To: <NurseSusie12>
Subject: Feeling Guilty!

Dearest Susie – I am guilty of being completely self-centred and self-absorbed; I have not even asked how your day has been. Also, it has just dawned on me that twice I have let you down when we were supposed to meet up. I must rectify this! In the meantime, would you be agreeable to giving me your phone number and I will call you. Can you believe it? We have not even spoken on the phone!! Yours, in anticipation xxx

Within a short space of time, Mitch received an email from Susie with her mobile phone number.

Susie was sitting down, clutching her mobile phone, and jumped when it rang. "Caller ID Withheld" was displayed on the screen. 'Hello,' said a warily-sounding Susie.

On the other end, Susie heard a deep well-spoken and well-modulated voice that caused her stomach to flip. 'Hello. Is that Susie?'

'Yes. It's me!' she replied, giggling slightly with nervousness. 'Is that you, Tim?'

'Yes, c'est moi! At last, we make contact, and can I say what a nice soft voice you have, Susie. It must be very soothing for your patients. So, how was your shift today?'

'Well,' Susie replied, 'one of our defibrillators stopped working. Then we had an emergency because we discovered there was an acute shortage of bandages on the ward, so I was sent on a "beg, borrow or steal" mission to the other wards, then Mrs Jones' sores…'

Mitch was bored and had to stifle a yawn. He must have dozed off because suddenly he could hear a shrill, 'Tim, Tim! Are you still there Tim?' in his ear.

'Yes, I'm still here, Susie. Your dulcet tones were lulling me to sleep. How lucky your patients are to have you caring for them. Your cool fingers soothing a fevered brow, your calm nature helping an anxious mother or distressed child. How I would love to put my head in your lap and have your healing hands stroke my hair.' *Bloody hell,* thought Mitch, *I'm getting a bit carried away here.* 'What do you say, Susie. Would you care for me?'

If Susie had harboured any doubts at all as to the authenticity of the person she knew as Tim, this phone call had allayed them. 'Of course I would, Tim. I'd love to care for you. To look after your every wish and need would give me pleasure. I would... Where are you calling from, Tim? I can hear a lot of noise.'

Mitch had been in a pub in Brighton on his laptop and had to go outside to make the phone call. There was the usual noise of traffic and people talking in the background, and he could use this to his advantage.

'Oh, didn't I tell you? I'm in the West End. Had a very productive meeting with my agent earlier, and now I'm off for a singing lesson as my agent thinks I should go into musicals, which would add another string to my bow. So, it's been lovely talking to you, my darling, but I must dash. Love you!' He disconnected, glad the charade was over because he had found it tiresome and tiring. He had done what he could and would now wait for Susie's response with regards to the money.

After the phone call, Susie felt elated. He had actually shown interest in her for a change and had hardly talked about himself at all, except towards the end. Feeling well disposed towards him and realising that their relationship had progressed to another level, she decided to call him and ask what the £10,000 was for as he hadn't mentioned it. She then realised that his number hadn't shown up and so she emailed him instead.

Mitch decided he would make her wait for his reply, as he didn't want to come across as too desperate for the money. Furthermore, he had made a huge effort speaking on the phone with her and it was not normally something he would do if the reward wasn't going to be that great.

It was the following morning when Mitch replied to Susie's email.

From: <TimStar1>
To: <NurseSusie12>
Subject: Hello!

Dearest Susie – Lovely talking with you yesterday. We must do it again, soon! As to the £10,000 – well, there are the flights with BA and I simply must travel business class on the flight out because they have flatbeds, and I must arrive refreshed, and then I must buy myself some decent clothes. I tried to get a credit card and was declined because I hadn't built up a sufficient credit score. Anyway, the credit limit, if I had been able to get a card, wouldn't have been enough. And then I tried to get a bank loan, but they said my earnings were too erratic, and I already have a small overdraft. So, I'm on the verge of giving up my dream. x

PS: My singing lesson went very well. She thinks I am pitch perfect, but my vocal range is limited and will probably need quite a few lessons. Don't think I can afford them. Feeling very glum atm.

Susie was about to do something that she would later regret.

From: <NurseSusie12>
To: <TimStar1>
Subject: Hello!

Darling Tim – Please don't be dispirited, and please don't give up! I can help you. I have some money saved up, and I can get a small loan from the bank. So, I will lend you the £15,000. I know you'll repay me. Not everyone gets a chance to live their dream, and if I can help you achieve yours then that will make me very happy. Shall I transfer it to your bank account? Lots of Love, Susie xxx

From: <TimStar1>
To: <NurseSusie12>
Subject: How are you?

Oh, Susie! My angel. My darling. How can I ever repay you? You have set me on the road to stardom and I will forever be in your debt. What a wonderful time we will have living in Los Angeles. Where shall we live? Bel Air? Beverly Hills? Or by the beach in Santa Monica? Attending the Oscars together, driving around in an open-top Cadillac and meeting all sorts of interesting and famous people. No more bedpans or grumpy patients for you, Susie. Can you transfer the money into the account of my agent here in the UK, so that the bank doesn't take some of it? The account is in the name of M. Mitchelson, and I'll text you the bank details. How can I ever thank you enough, Susie? Once I've booked my flights, I'll let you have all the details, and you can come and see me off. I don't think I've told you this, Susie – I LOVE YOU! Ciao for now.

In the end, Susie transferred £17,000 to the account of M. Mitchelson, and sent a brief email to "Tim" telling him she had sent the money and added an extra £2000 towards his singing lessons.

MITCH

Mitch reflected that, if he hadn't been a brilliant con artist, he could have been a professional juggler as he always kept the metaphorical balls in the air and rarely, if ever, dropped one. He was also a juggler of hearts and unfortunately some of them did get broken.

He was currently driving up to Luton to see Marnie. The last trip up hadn't been that successful as she was definitely down in the dumps. He also noticed that she had put on quite a bit more weight and seemed to be drinking rather a lot of cans of ready-mixed gin and tonic. She was also moaning quite a lot; wanting to know when he was actually going to earn some money and when they could move to bigger and more comfortable accommodation. So, this trip was to give her some much-needed attention and buoy up her spirits. He could understand why she felt this way, but as he explained to her more than once that, in order to have the life they wanted, this meant they had to spend time apart and it would be worth the wait. Only a few more months of this current batch of "projects", and they'd be off again.

Stopping to fill up with petrol, he bought a bunch of flowers and hoped they would mollify her. He also needed to put some distance between where he was currently living in Sussex and going back to Luton gave him that distance. He had work to do on the internet, and the physical and geographical space gave him the necessary mental space. Mitch often liked to think in metaphors, and his favourite ones centred around juggling or fishing. If he dropped just one ball, then the whole lot risked crashing down, or if he didn't have the right bait, then the fish wouldn't bite. He needed to make Marnie aware of this too, as he didn't want too much pressure from her. She was malleable though. He had allowed her to catch him, and he knew that she would never throw him back in because she also knew what side her bread was buttered on. *Ha – there's another good old saying,* thought Mitch.

There was no allocated parking for the block of flats where Marnie was staying, and so Mitch parked his car on the road outside. He entered the front door to the building and climbed the stairs to the flat. Opening the door, he called out, 'I'm here Marnie.' Silence. 'I'm excited to see you.' Silence. 'Marnie, where are you?'

Sometime later, Mitch heard footsteps on the stairs, and the door opened to reveal a startled Marnie. 'Mitch, I didn't expect you so soon. What a nice surprise.'

'Where have you been, Marnie?'

'I've been at the local primary school helping the kids with their reading. Do you know, Mitch, some of them can hardly read. It's very sad. Some of the parents don't read to them at home or get them to practice. And Mrs Hibbert—'

'Who is Mrs Hibbert?'

'Mrs Hibbert is the form teacher. Mrs Hibbert told me that some of the children go home to an empty house, even though they are very young, because the parents – and sometimes there's only one parent – are having to work all the time. It's really sad, Mitch.'

'Marnie, this is very laudable of you but I thought I told you to keep a low profile. I've explained to you time and time again that we must be inconspicuous at all times. I can see you're getting quite attached to the children, which will make it hard for you when we have to leave. And I don't want you getting too friendly with this Mrs Hibbert either. Do you understand?'

'Yes of course I understand, Mitch. But 'm lonely and I get bored, and then I get depressed and start eating and drinking too much. It's all right for you swanning here, there and everywhere, getting up to God knows what with God knows who. It's only a few hours a week, and only in term time. Anyway, it gets me out of this dump, and the children are very sweet. They call me "Miss", or "Miss Marnie", and it makes me happy.'

'Okay, Marnie, calm down. I can see this means a lot to you. Look, I've bought you these flowers. Now, be a good girl and put them in water as they've wilted a bit. I've got work to do. In case you've forgotten, whilst you're enjoying yourself playing at being mother, I'm earning us money of which, now doubt, you will benefit from. And yes, Marnie, thank you for *not* asking - I'd love a cup of tea.'

When Mitch had accused Marnie of playing at being mother, she felt that this was a highly insensitive and cruel remark to make, particularly as it was because of him they had never had children. When Marnie had met Mitch, and he had asked her to marry him within a short space of time, he had made it very clear that having children was out of the question. *The life I'm going to give you*, he had said, *will be spontaneous and involve a lot of travel. It will be exciting and adventurous.* 'Are you up for it?' he asked. 'Because it's not the kind of life suitable for children. Too much uprooting, and changing schools,' he explained.

Marnie, who had felt that she was lucky to have attracted someone like Mitch, had replied, 'I'm up for it, Mitch. So, no children.' She had, nevertheless, hoped that he would change his mind. He hadn't.

EDITH

Edith logged on to the over 60s dating website that Glenys had recommended. Although a bit of a dinosaur when it came to mobile phones, Edith had taken an interest in the IT classes at the school and knew a bit more than the basics. She had also, as part of her responsibility as a headmistress, taken a few online courses in database management, producing spreadsheets and completing online forms. *I may be a bit behind the times,* she thought, *but I'm not totally extinct yet.*

The first thing she did was to upload a photograph of herself. Not naturally photogenic, and by nature rather prim-looking, she found a recent one of her standing in front of the open-air theatre on the Rottingdean seafront. She stood at a slight angle, so that the friend who took the photograph managed to get a glimpse of the sea in the picture. It was quite windy that day, and slight ripples could be seen on the water, which Edith felt made the photograph look atmospheric. She imagined she was Sarah Woodruff, who was a character in John Fowles' novel, *The French Lieutenant's Woman,* who could often be found standing at the end of the jetty in Lyme Regis, staring out to sea. She had chosen to wear a flowery dress to give the impression of femininity, and wore a slight smile on her face, which she imagined made her look a touch mysterious. She was not a showy person and did not wear make-up; her mother drumming into her repeatedly that only "tarts, Edith, wear make-up. You have a natural beauty. Just remember that". So, Edith always made sure she looked neat and presentable.

Next, she tackled her profile but forgot Glenys' advice about not giving too much personal information away.

Name: Edie (Edith, she thought, seemed too severe. Edie, on the other hand, sounded young and vibrant. Racy, perhaps, like Warhol's Factory Girl – Edie Sedgewick – and then remembered that she had been too racy and got herself into all sort of problems. *Oh, blow it. You only live once*, she decided).

Age: 65 (*A bit of a big fib, but with dear Mother no longer around to tell me my nose will grow if I tell lies, who will find out*).

Location: East Sussex. Would like to meet a man of similar age, or older, for companionship. I am a retired professional with a lot of time on my hands. I am financially solvent, own my own property, and would describe myself as well-educated and cultured. So, please no tattoos, shaved heads, or football enthusiasts.

I am looking for someone with shared interests, such as the theatre, opera, walking and even holidays. As you can see from my photograph, I am not glamorous, but I do take pride in my appearance. If it's someone who wears a lot of make-up and dresses provocatively whom you're seeking, then I'm not for you.

Edith signed out of the site, with feelings of excitement, anticipation and anxiety comingled.

MITCH

Whilst Marnie was making Mitch a cup of tea, and feeling hurt by his comments, Mitch had gone into the bedroom, set up his laptop on the dressing table, and logged on to the internet. He was trying a new dating site he had come across which was aimed at retired professional people. Trawling through, he quickly discarded those who held little appeal for him for various reasons, and then shortlisted those who were "possibly-maybes". He came across one woman who gave her age as 65 and described herself as retired and financially solvent. In Mitch's experience, this usually meant that the person had money. He further read that she also owned her own property and was looking for a male companion. This particular profile, then, ticked many of his boxes. He chuckled at her photograph, because it was obvious to him that here was someone who was desperately trying to give the impression of mysterious allure because her pose showed her to be stood outside with a slightly stormy sea in the background, and her hair blown back from a face which could only be described as plain. Furthermore, she had raised one hand to her forehead, as if she was looking out to sea in search of someone.

Mitch decided to have a bit of fun with this one and knew exactly which of his personas he was going to employ. It was also clear to him that she was new to the dating game because of the personal information she had revealed, and also because she had left the field wide open for her profile to be seen internationally. He knew, from long experience, that the more dating-savvy limited the scope of their profiles to the UK or locally to where they lived. This didn't mean that there weren't con men or con women in the UK; far from it, because Mitch himself was one, but exposing themselves to the overseas community was a recipe for disaster, and one that Mitch could now take advantage of.

Cracking his fingers and stretching his arms over his head as a way of loosening up, he set to work. Just as he was about to start typing, Marnie came in with his tea and plonked it down in front of him, spilling some in the saucer. Not to be drawn into one of her sulks, Mitch simply said, 'Thanks, love. I'm at work now, so why don't you pop off to the shops and get us something nice for dinner.'

First, he uploaded a photograph of himself. Today, he was posing as an Arab sheikh having bought a white sheet and black headband whilst on a shopping trip in Brighton. He had also applied some face tan earlier which was now beginning to darken. Since meeting up with Fiona, he had grown a fuller beard and added a moustache. He had also applied a dark brown colour to the flecks of grey. With his chocolate brown eyes, set beneath perfectly shaped eyebrows, a slightly fleshy nose, and full lips, he looked every bit like a handsome Arab sheik. He had a slight smile on his lips, as he didn't want to look as severe as pictures often portrayed Arabic men – unsmiling and stern. Once he was happy with the image, he uploaded it and set about sending a message to "Edie".

Hello Edie – I am Sheikh Omar El Sharm.
I am from the United Arab Emirates. I am a little younger than you as I am 60. In my country, age does not matter. It is beauty that counts and you, Edie, to me, are beautiful. You are an English rose. Your demeanour from your photograph is one of modesty and shyness, with a restrained sense of

style. I do not like these showy women, who reveal too much of their bodies and wear far too much make-up. I would like to know more about you, Edie, if you are interested in conversing with me. Now I must fly – my magic carpet awaits me. That is a little joke of mine, Edie. As we say in Arabic, until next time "wadaeaan habibi".

Thank goodness for translation sites, thought Mitch, and hoped that she didn't realise he was using a play on words with the Egyptian resort of Sharm el-Sheikh. He heard the door open and then shut. 'Is that you, Marnie?'

'Yes, Mitch,' she shouted from the kitchen, 'I went to the corner shop to get us something to eat. I bought a chicken and ham pie, mashed potatoes and tinned peas. Is that okay? Oh, and I got you a can of lager.'

'Yes, that's fine, Marnie, and thanks for the lager.'

What Mitch would have preferred was a filet steak, cooked rare, a crisp green salad and a glass of chilled Sancerre; something of quality rather than quantity. *Speaking of which,* he remembered, *I must ring Fiona. Now, she is quality.*

'Hi, Fiona. It's Dan. Do you fancy going out for dinner on Tuesday evening?'

……

'Great. I'll pick you up at 6:30, if that's not too early. Thought we'd have a drive out into the countryside, find a nice pub, and have a few drinks and a meal. I'll need your address, though.'

Just as he ended the call, Marnie came into the bedroom. 'Who was that you were talking to?'

'My landlady. Mrs B. Confirming that I need the room next week.'

*

Sunday evening came and it was time for Mitch to head back down south. Excited at the thought of seeing Fiona again, who he genuinely found attractive and good company, he kissed Marnie on the cheek. 'I'm sorry if I was a bit cross with you, Marnie. I know how difficult this must be for you when we're apart like this, but it's all for a good cause. *Our* cause, so that we can have a nice life together. As long as you don't get too attached to those kids, and going to the school helps pass the time, then you can continue with it for the time being.'

On Monday morning, with Fiona's address entered into his navigation system, Mitch went exploring. He had already driven around the roads stretching back from the seafront and identified the wealthy areas. Therefore, he was a bit disappointed when the directions took him along the seafront towards Hove, which mainly consisted of blocks of flats. He noticed that there was a mixture of those that needed exterior maintenance, and those that were kept in pristine condition. From one of his earlier searches on property websites, he discovered how expensive some of them were and particularly those that had sea views. He baulked at the extortionate service charges and ground rents that were also listed, which would have put many of the properties out of the reach of ordinary people. Finally, he arrived at the address Fiona had given him and was reassuringly surprised to see that the block Fiona lived in had a gated entrance. Not only that, but the block looked to be kept in immaculate condition with many of the apartments – he decided they were apartments, which sounded more upmarket than flats – having balconies with a sea view. He parked the car down a side road and walked towards the pebbly beach where he could see the block from the back. He noticed that the ground-floor apartments had direct access, by way of a gate, to their own private part of the beach. This told him that Fiona lived in an exclusive development. He rubbed his hands together and grinned. *This is looking most promising,* he thought.

EDITH

The excitement was too much to bear. Having plucked up the courage to join the internet dating site, Edith tried very hard not to become a slave to logging on all the time to see if she had any responses, but she found herself unable to think of or do anything else. *I'm going to log on just one more time today, and then I'll leave it alone until tomorrow*, she told herself. What she feared most was that no-one would reply. However, she was a touch shocked and thrilled to see that there were quite a few replies. What she couldn't understand was why so many of them were from abroad; mainly American servicemen fighting in countries with civil unrest. Whilst Edith had nothing against Americans, or people in uniforms, she couldn't understand why these men, who were much younger than her, would be interested in a woman old enough to be their mother and, in some cases, their grandmother. She thought that maybe they were missing their mothers and grandmothers and it made her feel sad, but not sad enough that she wanted to reply to them.

Of those who had contacted her who lived in the United Kingdom, she selected those whose faces she liked the look of, but shuddered at the poor command of English, bad grammar and spelling mistakes. She didn't like being called "babe" either, as it was such a common expression. She noticed that, of those whose profiles showed them to be English, quite a few of them wrote "would of" instead of "would have". She recalled a time when a girl had been sent to see her for not submitting some homework. The girl – she couldn't remember her name – had stood in front of her and said, 'Well, Miss Bonnington, I would of done my homework but I had a stomach ache.'

'Would *have*, dear, not would *of.*'

'Would of what, Miss?'

'I would *have* done my homework. Not would *of* done my homework. That is not the English we teach here.'

Edith remembered that the girl just looked at her blankly, and she knew she would have been better off talking to a brick wall.

So, when she saw a message from "Trev" who lived in Essex which said, *'Hey Edie – I would of liked to get to know you better, but distance would of been a problem for us'*, followed by a yellow circle with a sad face, she immediately disregarded him. That was something else she noticed – so many of the messages contained yellow circles with silly faces grinning and winking. (She later found out from Glenys that these were called emojis). No doubt this was now considered an acceptable and fashionable way of communicating, but Edith was old-school.

She paused at a photograph of a man in Arabic dress called Sheikh Omar El Sharm. He had nice, soft brown eyes, and he was handsome in a dark, Middle Eastern way. Her mother popped into her head. She had had a thing for the actor Omar Sharif and had taken Edith to see him in the film *Anna Karenina*. She had also been partial to the actor, Peter O'Toole, who had taken the lead role in the film *Lawrence of Arabia*. The Arab connection, even though Omar Sharif was Egyptian, struck a chord with Edith and she felt that perhaps her mother would approve of this man, and so she read his profile. He was clearly well educated, as his written English, grammar and spelling were all very good. Neither was his language too flowery or his expressions common. Furthermore, to be called an "English rose" showed someone with a poetic sensibility, which appealed to Edith. She was concerned, though, how on earth they could ever meet. She didn't even have a passport and couldn't imagine visiting the United Arab Emirates. Still, she mused, he might be nice to correspond with and they could have a long-distance friendship.

She also came across someone called Lionel who had responded to her, and who lived closer to home in Worthing and was the same age as her real age. He was pleasant-looking, and so she read his profile as well. It wasn't very interesting, a bit matter-of-fact and straight to the point. His English was also good, even if it was very formal, but it showed that he had been decently educated which was imperative for Edith. She read that he was looking for a companion who shared his liking for walks along the seafront, good food, and evenings out at the theatre or cinema. He didn't travel abroad as he much preferred to holiday in Britain, adding that Devon and the Scottish Highlands were two favourite places he liked to visit. He had also said he was a widower, still missed his wife as they had had a long and happy marriage, but still enjoyed female company. If she, "Edie" – and he had asked if her name happened to be Edith, which, he added, was a good, traditional English name – was interested in chatting some more, he would be happy to hear from her.

Edith thought Lionel seemed nice enough, if a bit dull. Sheikh Omar, on the other hand, looked exotic and exciting, and Edith decided that perhaps *Mother would not approve*. However, Mother was no longer around and when Edith looked at the soft brown eyes and the sheikh's dark, manly features, she experienced an unfamiliar stirring inside which was not unpleasant.

Thus, she put Lionel to one side and replied to Sheikh Omar.

Hello, Sheikh Omar. Thank you for contacting me. I must admit, I have never come across anyone from Arabia before. I can only imagine how different our backgrounds and cultural experiences must be. I doubt we will ever get to meet, as I don't have a passport, but I would be more than happy to have you as an online friend. What do you think about that? I should add, Omar, if I can be informal, that my mother liked the actor Omar Sharif.

Almost immediately, a reply came back, making Edith jump in her chair.

Dearest Edie – my heart did a little flutter when I saw you had replied to me. Your mother would have approved of me, I think. Did you know that Omar Sharif was Egyptian and not Arabic? I think my mother must have liked that actor too. Perhaps our mothers would have got on with each other. But tell me why, Edie, you think we will never meet. My dear Edie – I have my own private plane which is at my disposal whenever I want. It would be a short trip to see you but, forgive me – I think I am jumping the gun a bit, as you English say. For now, as you suggest, let us chat online and get to know one another a bit more. I see that you like the opera and theatre. Do you like horseracing? So much more to talk about. I wait with anticipation for your reply, lovely Edie. Yours, Omar (not an actor, only a sheikh) x

Edith was alarmed. He had signed off with a kiss. What did that mean? Did a man and woman sign off with a kiss if they had never met? It seemed a bit presumptuous to Edith. No, she decided, he was just being friendly and perhaps these Arabic men were a bit hot-blooded; the thought of which made Edith blush.

MITCH

At the end of the day, it was just a job. A means to an end, and it had its upside in that he could have a lot of fun, and why not. He had lost his moral compass many years ago; even before he met and married Marnie. Dear sweet, ever-grateful, plain, pudding-like Marnie. She would never leave him, always go along with his plans, and although she sometimes moaned, he could always win her over. She was his perfect foil. Did his choice of career ever cause him to feel guilty? Once, maybe, when he had fleeced his cousin out of money, but the feeling passed quickly. After all, she was wealthy and she was family. Weren't family supposed to help each other out in times of need? Well, he was in need – all of the time.

Pulling up outside of the gated entrance to the apartment block where Fiona lived, Mitch pressed the buzzer and the gates opened. He parked in a space reserved for visitors and rang the bell for her apartment. Almost immediately, the door opened and out she came. She was a vision in blue, and Mitch was quite taken aback at how lovely she was. For a brief moment, he wished they were going on a real date.

Taking the coastal road out of Brighton, Mitch drove to Newhaven and then took the road to Eastbourne that he had driven along on one of his research trips. A signpost gave the name of a country pub in a village which was just off the main road to Eastbourne. It had won a couple of awards and was a typical country pub with oak beams and a log fire, which created a cosy, warm and welcoming atmosphere. Mitch ordered a filet steak cooked rare, a green salad and sweet potato chips. Fiona had the same, except she liked her steak cooked medium. As Mitch was driving, and Fiona said she couldn't possibly drink a whole of bottle of wine, they drank wine by the glass; one for Mitch and two for Fiona. Although Mitch preferred a dry white wine such as Sancerre or Sauvignon Blanc, he decided to mirror Fiona's choice of a red Shiraz. For dessert, they both chose the tarte Tatin with vanilla ice cream.

Over dinner, Fiona told him about her unhappy marriage. How she had tried just about everything to hold the relationship together, but her husband had simply checked out on her emotionally and checked in with another woman. Fiona further revealed that she had made no difficulties for either party and had been "rewarded" (and here she pulled a face) with a decent settlement and money towards the purchase of a new property.

'So, I can't really complain, can I?' she said, shrugging her shoulders.

'You're a lovely woman, Fiona. I don't know why anyone in their right mind would treat you in such a way. I really don't.' Then, Mitch took hold of Fiona's hand and, raising it to his lips, gently kissed it.

All the time Fiona had been speaking, Mitch had been watching her closely. Apart from the slight pursing of her lips when she had talked about being "rewarded", he saw no other outward signs of bitterness or emotional distress. A brief glimpse of sadness, because he knew she was not a hard-hearted person, but nothing that would indicate that she would cause him problems in the future, such as seeking revenge, or that she would do anything melodramatic. The one thing he did not want was a death on his hands.

'I have a little present for you. I hope you like them.' Mitch gave Fiona the earrings he had purchased in Lewes.

'Oh, Dan, they're exquisite. Thank you. This design is very much in fashion at the moment.'

'Well, the girl who sold them to me did say that they were very "on trend".'

Fiona laughed. 'Well, it's unfashionable now to use the word "fashionable". Everything is "on trend" these days.'

The evening came to an end and Mitch was genuinely sorry, because he had truly had a great time. The bill stung a bit, especially as it had proved more expensive to drink wine by the glass rather than buying a bottle, but Fiona's offer to pay because, "after all, Mitch, you paid for lunch", was heartily declined. 'I wouldn't hear of it, Fiona. I've had a great evening with you.'

Parking outside her apartment, he turned towards Fiona. Tucking a strand of hair behind her ear, he gently stroked his thumb across her cheek. 'Lovely, lovely, Fiona. I don't want the evening to end. You are such good company, and the complete opposite to my ex-wife, who I still find difficult to talk about.'

'I've had a good time too, Dan. We get on so well, even though it's only been such a short time. I don't usually do this, but would you like to come up for a coffee?'

'I'd like that very much,' and he leaned in towards her and kissed her softly on the lips.

Exiting the car, they went up to her apartment which was on the second floor. Gesturing to the settee, Fiona told "Dan" to make himself at home, whilst she went and made the coffee. Mitch took the opportunity to have a good look at the living room. He had had an inkling that the apartment would be nicely furnished, and he wasn't disappointed. Cool, pastel colours gave the living room a restful appearance, with a cream leather L-shaped settee and two reclining chairs, adding a touch of luxury. A collection of arty-looking ceramics were placed on the surface of the pale wood sideboard, and oil paintings that were mainly seascapes and beach scenes were hung on the walls. He was impressed with the overall interior she had created. Here was someone with taste, style and, obviously, money. In another lifetime, or in a parallel universe, he could envisage a life with Fiona. *Fuck,* he thought. *I'm getting distracted.*

He could hear a clatter of cups and saucers, and the whistling of a kettle. He wandered into the kitchen, where he saw Fiona at the counter putting ground coffee into a cafetière. Coming up behind her, he put his arms around her waist. 'Your husband must have been mad to let you go. To have someone like you to come home to would be a dream come true.' And in that brief moment, he meant it.

Fiona turned with a smile on her face, but a look of wariness in her eyes.

'You think I'm flattering you, don't you?' he asked. 'Well, I am. Unashamedly so. I mean it. Who wouldn't want to come home to you? You're gorgeous. Now, Fiona, I'm going to kiss you, and properly this time.'

Coming up for air a few minutes later, and with Mitch making it obvious that he had enjoyed the kiss, Fiona threw caution aside and suggested he might like to stay over. 'It's fairly obvious, Dan, that you enjoyed the kiss,' she said with a laugh. 'Look, we're both adults and neither of us want the evening to end, so why don't you stay over? What do you say?'

'I say, yes please.'

The following morning, Fiona brought "Dan" a cup of tea in bed and reminded him that she did her voluntary stint that day for the charity she supported. As she was a "roving" volunteer, she told him that she was off to the

Worthing branch and, as she caught the bus because she didn't own a car, she had to make sure she didn't miss it. So, if he didn't mind, she would use the shower first whilst he drank his tea. Mitch had not expected that things would have progressed so quickly and was caught unprepared for the next part of his plan. However, this was an opportunity he couldn't pass up, and needed to act quickly. Whilst Fiona used the shower in the en suite, Mitch took himself off to the small WC in the hallway where he sat and waited.

Some minutes later, he heard Fiona calling him from the bedroom. 'Dan, where are you?'

'I'm in the hallway toilet,' he replied.

Fiona waited, but there was total silence. 'Dan, I've got to go, otherwise I'll miss the bus and won't make it on time to open up the shop. Are you okay?'

Going into the hallway, Fiona heard a retching sound, followed by a groan. 'I'm not well, Fiona. I've got a bad stomach. I've just vomited, and, well...' This was followed by more retching.

'Oh dear. How strange. We ate exactly the same food, and I'm fine.'

All of this posed a dilemma for Fiona. She was responsible for opening the Worthing shop that day, and she didn't like letting anyone down. So, she made a decision she would later regret because, after all, hadn't they spent the night together and "Dan" had asked her if she would like to go away for a weekend soon.

'Okay, Dan, don't worry. Take as long as you need. There's something for an upset stomach in the bathroom cabinet, and drink lots of water to rehydrate yourself. I'm off now. Let yourself out, and I'll ring you later.'

Mitch heard the door shutting and her footsteps on the stairs. Wasting no time, he went into the small bedroom which he knew doubled up as her study. He booted up her computer, which he knew was not password protected. The silly girl had let slip, during the meal the evening before, that she didn't have a password for her computer. He had engineered a discussion around computer hacking, security and keeping different passwords, by telling her a story of how someone had hacked into his bank account and stolen some money. If she was going to reveal anything of that nature to him, she would do it then and he would store the information for later use. She had played right into his hands, when she said, 'Oh, that's an awful story, Dan. Did you ever get the money back?'

'Sadly not. I just put it down to experience. Changed all my passwords for everything and am now extra vigilant.'

'Well, I probably shouldn't tell you this, but my computer isn't password protected. There's no need. No one is ever going to use it except me, so what's the point? As for using various passwords, I can hardly remember one and so I use the same for all of the sites I use. Is that a bit foolish?'

'It is a bit, Fiona. But I suppose you do have different memorable information for each site you use, in case it's asked for?'

She had shrugged her shoulders and replied, 'Nope. I use the same information. Also, everything is written down in my little black book.'

Silly, silly girl, thought Mitch, as her screen lit up and he went to the folder marked "documents". Here he found a subfolder marked "Investments". Opening it up, he saw that she had a healthy portfolio. He also found three further subfolders for three different banks, which again showed healthy balances. He began to perspire slightly. It always made him nervous when in the initial stages of accessing someone else's financial records. He connected to the internet and typed in the name of the first bank into the browser. The bank's main website came up, and Mitch proceeded to the log in section. Very helpfully, Fiona had stored her username and so it appeared automatically in a string of asterisks. Next came the prompt for the password and memorable information. Opening the desk drawer, he found her "little black book" which was her euphemism for an address book where she stored her information. Turning to the page for the first bank, she had very helpfully written down all the information he needed to access her account. Going through his routine of cracking his fingers, and stretching his arms above his head, which signalled the start of serious work, he got into her bank account very easily. She also had a savings account, and both were healthily in funds.

He did the same for the next bank and that account was also well into the black. It was only the third bank where she held an account that scuppered him. In order to access that account, a card reader and bank card were required. He found the reader, but Fiona would have had the card in her purse. Without that, he couldn't get access as there were too many extra checks to go through. In any event, what he had discovered was more than enough for his needs. He made a note of her banking details for future use and closed down the computer. Going down the stairs whistling the tune to "We're in the Money", he let himself out. From the car, he called Fiona and thanked her for being so understanding and accommodating, and that he would be in touch soon with details for their weekend away.

EDITH

Edith and Sheikh Omar had been messaging each other on the dating site on a regular basis. He had uploaded more photographs showing a picture of his palace, his camels, and a photograph of a solitary Bedouin tent in the desert. The message that was attached to this last photograph had alarmed Edith. The sheikh had suggested that she come and visit him, and he would put her on his favourite camel and whisk her way to the desert. Edith had replied, feeling somewhat relieved, that she couldn't travel abroad as she didn't have a passport. Not to be deterred, Sheikh Omar had replied that, as he had his own plane, he would fly her to him and, as she would be treated as a VIP guest in his own country, they could probably get around that issue. Edith had countered, and was amazed at how quick-thinking she was, that, regrettably, she was afraid of flying. Sheikh Omar had responded with a simple "Then I'll come to you".

Edith was beside herself with excitement. In fact, she was in a complete tizz and phoned her friend, Glenys, for advice. 'What shall I do? What do I do if he doesn't like me, after coming all this way? What shall I wear?'

'Now, Edith, you really must calm down. Of course he'll like you. What's not to like? He's seen your photograph, you've been chatting for a while, and he's obviously keen to meet you. As for what to wear – wear what you always wear. Something flowery. Oh, and you'll have to buy some silky underwear. We can go into Brighton and have a look in Victoria's Secret.'

Edith, who much preferred the feel of brushed cotton and winceyette next to her skin, shuddered at the thought.

That morning, Edith had received a message from the sheikh:

My dearest Edie – if I may call you "dearest". Exciting news. I am coming to England next week and would love to meet up with you face to face. What do you say?

Dear Sheik Omar: Oh, my goodness! I cannot believe that. I would very much like to meet you. I should tell you, though, that my name is Edith, but you can still call me Edie.

Dear Edith – Edith is a good English name, and you can call me Omar now that we are more familiar with each other. I will be flying in on my private plane to the South Terminal at Gatwick. It is white and gold, with a falcon on the tail. I have my very own private pilot. He's British (all the best pilots are British) and he is called Malcolm Mitchelson. Aren't you impressed, Edith? I will contact you with the date of my arrival, nearer the time. Perhaps, now, Edith, we can talk to each other over the phone, if you don't mind giving me your phone number. Oh, and, Edith, I hope you have some nice dresses. I will be taking you to the opera at Glyndebourne, and Charleston where the Bloomsbury Group lived and painted. We will have an English cream tea – scones, jam and cream. Oh, and horse racing at Goodwood and Ascot. I forgot to tell you I have my own stable of Arab stallions. They are thoroughbreds (just like me) and

*going racing is a favourite pastime of mine. You may
need to buy a new hat. Perhaps two!! X*

At the mention of stallions and thoroughbreds,
Edith had felt very hot and had to fan her face with
both hands. She also experienced the unfamiliar stirring
again in her stomach, which had begun to creep further
downwards.

*Oh my goodness, Omar. I am feeling giddy with
excitement. How is it that you know all about these
places if you have never visited England before?*

*Edith, dearest – did I say I haven't been to England
before? Au contraire, I know England very well. Did
I not tell you that I went to school in England – to
Eton, and then to Cambridge where I studied the
Classics, achieving a double first.*

Mitch had been forced to disconnect after this last
statement because he was laughing so hard. *More like a
double-D in my case*, he thought and a fleeting image of
buxom Bev popped up. Edith, on the other hand, had
got flustered. In her mind, Glyndebourne, Charleston,
Goodwood and Ascot loomed large. She would have
to buy some clothes and accessories and decided to
ask her friend Margaret, who was less flighty and flirty
than Glenys, to accompany her.

Sitting outside a café in the marina, the sun shone,
and Edith felt very happy and carefree. Having brought
her friend up to date, she was surprised by her response,
which was not quite as expected.

'Edith, this all sounds a bit far-fetched, if you don't
mind me saying. Please don't take this the wrong way,
dear, but you're not exactly a pin-up, are you?'

'No, Margaret, I know I'm not exactly a "pin-up", as you put it, but he has behaved perfectly respectful and polite in his messages to me. His command of English is impeccable, and there has been nothing smutty in his conversation.'

'But why would a rich Arab sheikh, who lives in a palace, and have his own plane, be interested in you?'

'Well, Margaret, not everyone wants a dolly bird for a lady friend. There are still some men who want a modest, ladylike, gentlewoman, who knows how to conduct herself in polite society and not get drunk and fling herself at other men!' Edith could feel herself getting annoyed, whilst simultaneously wondering if there weren't kernels of truth in what her friend was saying.

Margaret gave an unladylike snort. 'Oh, be realistic, Edith. How do you know what he says is true? Anyone can say they went to Eton and Cambridge, and anyone can put up photographs that they've found on the internet. It all seems too good to be true, if you ask me.'

'Well, I'm not asking you. Glenys believes he's real, and she's being very supportive. I was going to ask you to come shopping with me, but I think I'll invite her instead.' Edith made a mental note to keep Glenys away from the racy lingerie shops.

'Now, now, Edith. Of course I'll come shopping with you. I just don't want to see you get hurt, or worse, scammed out of your money. And anyway, Glenys is not a good judge of character. Look at that date she went on recently, where he asked her if she was into S and M, and at her age! Disgusting.'

'What's S and M?'

'Oh, honestly, Edith. You're like a lamb to the slaughter.'

'Now you're just being mean,' replied Edith, feeling equally annoyed and upset. Speaking slightly hysterically, she added, 'And he's not after my money. He's got enough of his own. And, anyway, I've got his mobile number, so I can ring him whenever I want.'

'Go on then. I dare you.'

'I can't do that. He'll think I'm one of those forward, pushy women. My mother, God rest her soul, always said, "Edith, you must never run after a man, otherwise they will get the wrong idea. You must always let the man do the running".'

'I'll ring him then. Give me the phone, and I'll ring the number.'

'No, I'll ring him. I don't trust you. You might say something to put him off.'

Edith rang the number she'd been given, but a recorded message played:

This is Sheikh Omar El Sharm. I can't come to the phone right now, but please leave me a message and I will get back to you. Edie, if this is you calling me, it won't be long until we meet in person.

The voice Edith heard was deep and cultured, with a slight trace of an accent which she couldn't place. Hearing his voice, and the personal message he had left for her, caused her heart to beat slightly faster.

'It went to voicemail, but he left me a personal message.'

'Anyone can leave—'

But Margaret was cut off mid-sentence by Edith who got up suddenly and announced she was off shopping, 'By myself!'

As Edith headed for the bus stop to catch a bus into Brighton, she wondered how it was that a day which had started so well and made her walk with a spring in her step, had rapidly gone down-hill, making her mood gloomy and her legs heavy. It wasn't only the discussion with her friend that had caused this, although much of it was, but a niggling feeling Edith had that something wasn't quite right. It was to do with the mobile phone number he had given her. On occasion, Edith had found it necessary to call certain pupils' parents who lived abroad. She knew, therefore, that when calling overseas, there was always a slight delay for the call to be connected, and that the ringtone was different. When she called the number Sheikh Omar had given her, which she saw had a UK country code, the ringtone was the same as for the UK and the call went straight through to voicemail.

Subconsciously, these things concerned Edith, but she brushed them aside thinking that there was probably a very good explanation.

MITCH

It was Friday morning and Mitch was feeling a bit stressed. He would soon have to bring his current batch of projects to a close, and this always involved some fine-tuning with no room for mistakes of any sort. The gamble with the phone call to Nurse Susie had paid off, and he saw that she had transferred the money. He had been pleasantly surprised to see that she had added a bit extra and patted himself on the back for thinking up the story about singing lessons. He deleted his online profile and crossed her off his list of projects. He also had to finalise things with Edith and move Project Fiona onto the next stage.

There had also been an unexpected bonus with his landlady. The more he got to know Dorothy, the more he realised that she was a kind and trusting person who had taken a real liking to him. She had often spoken about her "dear departed George" and how much he – "Daniel" – reminded her of George. For his part, Mitch had not given her too much personal information except to occasionally mention that he had a son who was not very well. Dorothy had expressed concern and offered to help in any way she possibly could. Mitch was about to take her up on her offer. Having already laid the groundwork, it was time to bring his plan to fruition. So, he had a lot to do and now, he had to dash off to Luton again to see Marnie. Shouting a goodbye to Dorothy, he shut the door and sped off. It was going to be an exhausting few days, but worth it. Not forgetting, of course, to include a bit of fun to lighten his heavy load.

DOROTHY

Dorothy had just sat down at the kitchen table to have her morning cup of coffee when her landline rang in the hallway. Answering it, she was surprised to hear a very flustered Daniel on the other end.

'Oh, thank God I caught you, Mrs B. I'm at Cobham Services and it's too far to come back. Could you do something for me please? I think I left my laptop on, and I'm worried about hacks and viruses. You can't be too careful these days.'

'Oh, hello, Daniel. Are you not at Shoreham or Newhaven today?'

'No, Mrs B. I've had to go home a bit earlier today, and I left in such a rush that I'm sure I've left my laptop on.'

'Oh, okay. Erm, you know I'm not very good with computers as I don't have one. But I'll try if you can tell me what I need to do.'

'It's very easy, Mrs B. All you have to do is look for the letter X in the top right-hand corner. That will close the page down. Then, in the bottom left-hand corner, you'll see four squares which make up one big square. Click on that, and then look for the shape that resembles a door knocker. Click on that, and then press "shut down". All you have to do then is close the lid. Is that clear?'

'Yes, I think I can manage all that. Will you hold on whilst I do it?'

'My battery is low, Mrs B. I'm sure you'll be fine.' And he rang off.

Hurrying to the back of the bungalow where Daniel's bedroom was, she entered the room. It was, she was pleased to see, very neat and tidy. Having only been in his room once since he moved in, because he had said he would take care of the cleaning as he didn't want to put her to any trouble, she took a moment to look around. Two photographs were displayed on the side table; one showed a smiling couple and a young boy in a garden, whilst the other was of the same family at the seaside, with the young boy sat on a donkey.

She then went over to the desk where the open laptop was situated. Before closing down the page, she took a quick look. There was a heading which read, "TO-DO LIST FOR WEE DANNY". She knew she was being nosy but couldn't help looking. She noticed that Daniel had listed a number of things to do. *(1) Set up "crowdfunding" page for continued treatment. (2) Send thank you letters for donations already given. (3) Contact bank re: loan. (4) Enquire about second mortgage. (5) Chase up equity release enquiry.* Somewhat puzzled by what she had read, Dorothy nevertheless closed down the page and saw that the screen was taken up with a picture of the same family, but this time the young boy was in a wheelchair and looked to be very disabled. Dorothy closed the screen down and shut the lid of the laptop. She couldn't believe what she had discovered. Her lodger, Daniel, who was the nicest man she had ever met – after her husband, of course – had mentioned that his son was ill, but he hadn't said that he was severely disabled. Not only that, it became clear to Dorothy that he was going to get himself into all sorts of debt by borrowing money, and possibly jeopardising his family home.

Returning to the kitchen, she had only just sat back down to drink her coffee, which had now grown cold, when the landline in the hallway rang again. "What now?" she said with a big sigh. Whoever was calling had not listed their number, and normally she would ignore such calls. This time, however, she made an exception, and was greeted with a cheery male voice with a broad Yorkshire accent.

'Good morning. Can I speak to Mr Daniel Simpson, please. Tell him it's David Banning from Release Your Equity, in response to his enquiry.'

'Oh! Well Daniel isn't here. He's gone home for the weekend.'

'Do you know when he will be back?'

'Well, it's usually Sunday evening or Monday morning. Have you tried his mobile?'

'Yes, just now. It's switched off. So, I thought I'd try this number. It's the alternative one he listed on the form.'

'Well, Daniel doesn't live here all the time. Only Monday to Friday. He's my lodger. Have you tried his home number?'

'He only gave this number and a mobile. Look, no problem. I'll try again in a few days. Just tell him that I've received his enquiry about releasing equity in his house, and I'll consider the options and get back to him. I'm sorry to have troubled you. Thanks for your time.'

Dorothy was a bit shocked and couldn't quite get to grips with what was happening. In a daze, she began to make her way slowly back to the kitchen, but then the post fell through the letterbox and she turned and went to retrieve it. One of the envelopes was addressed to "Mr D. Simpson, c/o Mrs Dorothy Beresford". A return address on the back of the envelope indicated that the letter had come from a mortgage broker. Two things immediately came into Dorothy's mind: the first was that Daniel was obviously not telling his wife what he was up to which is why he had only listed Dorothy's landline number, and why mail was being addressed to him care of her address; the second was that she couldn't let this happen. There and then, she decided to lend him enough money to pay for his son's continued treatment, and to give Daniel and his wife some financial stability. As soon as he came back, she would give him a cheque and would not take "no" for an answer.

MITCH

Arriving back in Luton, Mitch gave Marnie a big hug and brought her up to date. Relieved that she seemed in better spirits than his last visit, he decided to take her out to dinner that evening. There was a Thai restaurant within walking distance, which meant he could have a few pints of lager. He was in such a good mood, and because Marnie was cheerful, he decided to take her shopping so that she could wear something new that evening. Basking in the attention she was getting from Mitch, she felt very well disposed towards him and allowed herself to be diverted away from the moderately expensive clothes shops and steered towards cheaper ones, where she found a reasonably priced dress and pair of shoes. Mitch also had some shopping to do. Because it had been necessary to leave his laptop behind, he now needed to buy a replacement. Luckily, he had found a shop that sold second-hand computers and laptops and purchased one at a reasonable price.

Later that afternoon, after much persuasion and nuzzling of her neck, Marnie allowed herself to be made love to, or, as Mitch rather unromantically described it, engage in a bit of "rumpy pumpy".

Marnie, who knew Mitch like the back of her hand, wondered at this sudden display of attention and generosity, and it immediately made her suspicious. She was to find out why later that evening.

Complimenting Marnie on how nice she was looking, which made her even more suspicious, they made their way to the restaurant. After a starter of spring rolls for

Marnie, and spicy sweetcorn cakes for Mitch, and whilst they waited for their Thai green chicken curry to arrive, Mitch took hold of Marnie's left hand. 'Marnie, my love, you know you are the only woman for me, don't you?'

Marnie sensed that she was about to be given a load of old flannel. 'Yes, Mitch, I suppose so. What is it you want me to do now?'

'Now, now, Marnie, don't be like that. You know that everything I do is for the both of us?'

'Of course I do. Out with it, Mitch.'

'I need your engagement ring.'

'What!' spluttered Marnie. 'You're married to me. That would make you a bigamist!'

'Don't be silly. I'm not getting married. I'm just getting engaged.'

The waiter came with their curries, two bowls of rice, and two pints of lager.

'This had better be worth it, Mitch Mitchelson. Do I get it back?'

'Probably not,' replied Mitch, scooping up some rice and curry. Seeing the thunderous look on Marnie's face, he quickly added, 'Marnie, I will buy you the biggest diamond engagement ring as a replacement.'

Yeah, right, thought Marnie to herself, as she handed it over.

Later that night, too full of curry and feeling fed up, Marnie rejected Mitch's advances and turned over to go to sleep. For his part, Mitch was very happy. Everything was falling into place nicely.

Up bright and early, Mitch went into the kitchen and made Marnie a cup of tea. Putting the tea on the bedside table, he gave her a kiss on the cheek, and then booted up the reconditioned laptop he had bought. It was very slow coming on, and the screen kept going blank, but finally he was able to get online. Logging on to the "seniors" dating site, he sent a message to Edith to say that he would be boarding his plane soon and to expect a call from him. He heard Marnie waking up and turned to talk to her.

'It won't be long now, Marnie. Just a bit more patience. Okay, my love? I was thinking, before I head back down south, we could go for lunch. I noticed a Harvester yesterday that did a carvery, and you could wear that pretty dress again that I bought you. What do you say?'

Marnie, who was not used to terms of endearment from Mitch, happily agreed.

It was Sunday afternoon and Mitch was driving back to Saltdean. He decided it was time to have some fun and called Edith on his hands-free phone. He hadn't checked to see if she had replied to his last message, because either way he knew he had successfully reeled her in. He also didn't have a clue about the time difference between the UAE and the UK but didn't feel that would be a problem either.

'Edith,' he shouted, 'It's Sheikh Omar here. Can you hear me?'

Edith could just about hear the sheikh over what seemed to be a lot of noise. She heard horns beeping and sirens. Sometimes Mitch really felt that lady luck was on his side. There had been an accident on the M1 which he put to full advantage.

'Can you hear the sirens, Edith, and the beeping of horns?'

'Yes, I can. Are you on a motorway? Has there been an accident?'

'No, Edith, my dear. That is my cavalcade. Whenever I travel anywhere, particularly if I am leaving the country, I am given a send-off and also escorted to the airport. I'm on my way to the UK, Edith, to see you. I'll be arriving tomorrow at 11 o'clock, Gatwick South. Will you be there to meet me?'

'Yes, yes, of course I will. I can't believe this is happening. I'm so happy, but also a bit nervous.'

'There is nothing to be nervous about, my dear Edith. We are going to have some lovely times together, and then we can see what the future brings. Have you ever slept in a Bedouin tent in the desert, with only the camels and stars for company? Oh, I forgot, and me, of course.'

'Oh my goodness,' said Edith, completely swept up in the romance and drama of the situation.

'Well, my English rose, you are in for a very big surprise. Now I must go. See you soon.'

Mitch disconnected from the phone and turned on the radio. David Byrne was singing, 'I'm wicked and I'm lazy. Oh, won't you come and save me.' Mitch chuckled to himself. He was certainly wicked, but no one could accuse him of being lazy, and he sang along at the top of his voice.

The accident on the M1 had slowed his journey down, and he arrived back in Saltdean later than expected. Parking his car outside the bungalow, he let himself in. As soon as the door closed behind him, Dorothy came rushing into the hallway waving a cheque at him.

'Daniel, you must take this. I insist. I don't need the money. I'd like you to have this.'

'Whatever is the matter, Mrs B? Let's go and sit down, and you can tell me what the problem is.'

Dorothy continued to hover in the hallway. 'Well, when you called the other day and asked me to turn off your laptop, I couldn't help but notice, erm, the "to-do" list you had made.'

'Have you been taking a sneaky peak, Mrs B?' enquired Mitch with a smile on his face. He could see that she was slightly discomfited because her face had reddened, as if she had been caught out doing something underhand.

'I'm sorry, Daniel. I cannot lie. When you asked me to turn off your laptop, I saw the page and then, on the screen, a picture of you, your wife, I presume, and your son. So… Well, yes, I admit it. I didn't know that your son was that poorly, or that you had financial worries.'

'I'm a private person, Dorothy, and why would I want to burden you with my problems. Me and the wife try to stay strong for wee Danny's sake, and we also try to stay independent. We've learnt that people, even our own family, aren't that supportive.'

'What is wrong with your son?'

'Danny has a muscle-wasting condition. There's no cure for it, but we've found an expert in the States who has had remarkable results in slowing down the physical deterioration. It's just so expensive, though, and we don't have that kind of money. Also, with the NHS in the dire straits it's in at the moment, we're not sure how much longer we can get the necessary free treatment or medication for Danny. As you discovered, I'm in the process of setting up a "gofundme" page, but so many people are doing that nowadays that I don't hold out much hope really. And you've seen the rest of my ideas, but it's all a bit disheartening.'

'Well, then, Daniel, I'm glad I snooped,' said Dorothy, with a satisfied grin on her face. 'Take this cheque. It will be more than enough, I think, to cover the expenses and medical bills. I've left the payee section blank for you to complete.'

'This really is very generous and kind of you. I will, of course, pay you back. I don't know when exactly, but you can trust me.'

'I know I can, Daniel. I am so pleased I've been able to help.'

'Well, I must bid you goodnight, Dorothy. It's been a long day, and a slightly overwhelming one at that. I've got a busy day tomorrow and need some shuteye. Again, I can't thank you enough.'

Taking the cheque, Mitch left Dorothy standing in the hallway and went to his bedroom. Putting the cheque in an envelope and addressing it to Marnie, with a note telling her to pay it into the bank account she had kept in her maiden name of Simpson at the beginning of the following week, he then went into the bedroom and shaved off his moustache and trimmed his beard down to a designer stubble.

In the meantime, Dorothy had returned to her living room very pleased that she had done someone a good deed. She put the letter from the mortgage broker in her waste bin, and also decided not to tell "Daniel" about the telephone call, not realising, of course, that it had, in fact, been her lodger calling.

It was Monday morning and Mitch woke up very early. He had found it difficult to get to sleep because, when he was involved in an elaborate scam, he went over all the fine details in his mind, over and over again. Plus, he was full of nervous energy. He tiptoed along the hallway and quietly let himself out of the front door. Posting the cheque to Marnie in the post box at the end of the road, he unlocked his car and drove towards Gatwick Airport. He called Edith again and, although it was still early morning, he was certain she would be up because, like him, but for very different reasons, she wouldn't have been able to sleep either.

As Mitch had rightly predicted, Edith had indeed been up early. She had managed to drink a cup of tea, but her nerves were doing somersaults in her stomach, and she didn't feel confident that she would keep any breakfast down because she felt queasy. She also had her journey to plan. She didn't drive; in fact, she had never learnt to drive and had always relied on buses and trains. In special circumstances, she took a taxi. She was dithering over whether to book a taxi, or plan her journey by bus and train, when her phone rang, and it was Sheikh Omar.

'Edith,' he shouted. 'It is Omar. Excuse my shouting, but I am trying to talk over the noise of my plane's engine. I am looking forward to seeing you. Finally, I will get to meet you face to face and to witness your lovely smile. I have a slight problem, though, which is causing me some embarrassment.'

'Oh, good morning Sheikh Omar. How are you? I'm just planning my journey to the airport.'

'Edith, you don't need to call me sheikh anymore. From now on, it is Edith and Omar.'

Edith could feel herself blushing, and at a loss for words. *Edith and Omar, Edith and Omar,* she replayed over and over in her mind.

'Are you there, Edith?'

'Yes, I'm here, Sheikh… Erm, I mean, Omar.'

'Did you hear what I said, Edith? I have a problem, but I am embarrassed by it.'

'Oh no! What is it? What's wrong? Can I help?'

'I'm not sure you can help, unless you have £20,000, which I'm sure you don't. Who does have that kind of money these days, except me, of course? Look, I'm going to have to ring off. The control tower is calling again. I'll call you soon. Don't worry. I'm sure I can sort something out.'

Whilst Edith was now fretting over this latest call, and unable to sit still, Mitch had pulled into a side road near the airport. Planes could be heard taking off and landing, and he wound down the window just enough for the noise to be heard. Calling Edith again, he explained his problem.

'The thing is, Edith, and it's very stupid, but I don't carry any money on me. Everything is organised for me in my country, and all I have to do is sign for things. I had assumed that my personal assistant would have arranged all of the financial aspects for my trip to the UK. Then I learnt, as I was about to land, that nothing had been paid for or organised. When I get back to my country, I will dismiss him from my employment and then he will have to explain to his wife why they don't have enough money to feed their children, of which there are many. And now, Edith, you will think me a very hard-hearted person, but his incompetence has caused me a huge problem.'

'Oh dear! Please don't fire him. Think of the children. Tell me what the problem is, and perhaps I can help.'

On the other end of the phone, Mitch pretended to huff and puff. 'When you land a plane at an airport, there are all kinds of costs involved. Landing costs and refuelling costs. Hangar fees. airport duty and so on. I had assumed that all of this had been organised and paid for, up front. But it hasn't, and my pilot has now been told he cannot land the plane until there are assurances in place that these fees will be settled immediately. There you have it. So here I am, sitting in a plane, way up in the sky, literally going round in circles.'

'How much do you need, Omar?

'I need £20,000, as soon as possible.'

Although Edith had never been on a plane, and rarely went to an airport, she knew that it must involve huge sums of money, and if that plane was privately owned, she could only imagine how expensive it would be. So, she had no qualms in offering him the money. 'I can let you have that. I could do a bank transfer, but because it will be going overseas, it may take more than a day.'

'Yes, I realise that. I wonder if you would mind, then, transferring the money into my pilot's bank account which is in the UK, and which should clear within two hours. His name, as I told you, is Malcolm Mitchelson and his account is in the name of Mr M. Mitchelson. Could you do that for me, Edith, and then let me know when the transaction has gone through so that I can let the relevant airport ground staff know?'

'Of course, Omar. I'll get on to it straight away.'

'Thank you I'll text you the details now. You are my guardian angel, and I am sending you down a kiss from the clouds.'

Because Edith's bank where she lived had long closed down, her nearest one was a bus journey away into Brighton. Thus, she had been forced to get to grips with internet banking, which was now standing her in good stead. She had an account with two different banks and transferred the money in two lots. Both banks had a pop-up alert asking if she knew who she was transferring the money to, and only to proceed if it was secure to do so. Whilst Edith, in all honesty, could not really say she did know the person she was sending the money to, because they had never met in person, she nevertheless reassured herself that she would be meeting him soon and pressed the "proceed" button. A message popped up after both transactions to advise that the money should arrive in the recipient's bank account within two hours. Ringing the mobile number she had for the sheikh, she left a message to say that she had transferred the money.

As regards to her trip to the airport, she had decided that she would take the bus into Brighton Station, and then catch the Gatwick Express. Omar had said he would be landing at 11:00, but she assumed he would be a bit late because of his current difficulties. It was whilst she was putting the final touches to her appearance, and deciding which coat to wear, that her phone rang again. It was Sheikh Omar.

'Hello, Edith. Thank you for your message. I am now faced with another problem. I have been allowed to land but am now being held by customs. It is a total disaster. I had brought you gifts of gold and a few diamond trinkets, but it seems they are over the limit and I must pay airport duty on them or else they will all be confiscated. If that isn't bad enough, because I do not have any English currency on me, they say they will not allow me to enter the United Kingdom until I can prove I have sufficient funds for my stay here. I cannot believe this country of yours, Edith. I have told them that all I want to do is to see my fiancé, and that they are preventing me from doing this. I am beside myself with worry.'

Edith, who felt that perhaps matters had suddenly overtaken her as she hadn't agreed to getting engaged, nevertheless went ahead and asked what else she could do for him.

'What I need, now, in order to enter the United Kingdom, and to be able to bring in these gifts for you, is to pay customs £10,000, which will cover the duty and show that I have sufficient funds whilst I am in the country. Is it at all possible that you can get this sum of money in cash? I can't leave the customs detention area, and, I ask you, is this any way to treat a Saudi prince? So could you get hold of this sum and hand it over to my pilot? Please, Edith. I am begging you.'

Caught up in the drama of the moment, and concerned that he might now be having second thoughts about his visit because of the difficulties he was experiencing, Edith did not question how a sheikh could suddenly morph into a prince and told him that she would go to the bank forthwith and do her best to get the cash he needed.

'Thank you, Edith. You are my saviour. When we meet, perhaps you will allow me to plant a gentle kiss on those lovely lips of yours.'

Edith, whose mother had drummed into her that a girl should always play hard to get, answered primly, 'We'll see about that, Omar.' However, Mitch detected a smile in her voice.

*

Getting the £10,000 in cash proved a lot more difficult than transferring £20,000. Catching the bus into Brighton, she headed into her bank. The young teller behind the counter noticed that the elderly woman standing in front of her looked nervous and kept fidgeting with the carrier bag she was holding. Looking at Edith closely, the young bank teller asked her if she had been pressurised into handing over this money, to which Edith replied, 'No, not at all.'

The young woman then asked Edith what the money was for; was it for an upfront payment for building work, or had she been brought to the bank by someone purporting to be from the police or a courier working for the police.

'No, not all,' Edith replied, feeling irritated. 'Look, young lady, I know you're only doing your job, but I'm not some silly old woman who's lost her marbles. Now, I'm in a bit of a rush, and I'd like my money please.'

The young girl looked at Edith and sighed. 'I will just need to check with the manager to get this amount signed off, as I don't carry that much money in my drawer.'

Having finally managed to get the money and, due to the fact that time was slipping by, combined with the nervous state Edith found herself in as she had neither seen nor handled so much money before, she decided to catch a taxi to the airport. As instructed, the driver dropped her outside the entrance to the South Terminal and Edith made her way to the arrivals hall. She was late, but saw no one who resembled Sheik Omar or anyone, for that matter, who looked remotely Arabic or wearing traditional Arabic clothes. She then remembered that he was being held by customs. Her phone beeped to notify her that a message had arrived. It read: *Still detained. Don't know for how long. Pilot will come and greet u on my behalf. C u soon. O x*

Edith turned away from the meeting area, deciding whether or not to get a coffee. A man, who looked vaguely familiar, was walking straight towards her. He looked a bit like the sheikh, except he didn't have a full beard or moustache. He was wearing navy blue trousers, black shoes, and a navy-blue jumper, under which was a white shirt and navy-blue tie. In his left hand he carried what looked like, to Edith, a pilot's hat, and in his right hand he held a bunch of red roses. Edith looked around her to see if there were any attractive women standing nearby, thinking he might be heading towards one of them, but, no – he was coming directly towards her.

'You must be Edith? I'm Malcolm, Sheikh Omar's private pilot. He said you would be expecting me and asked me to say that he's sorry he can't be here to personally greet you, but he's been unavoidably delayed.'

Edith was feeling a bit flustered, but also excited at being the centre of attention. She could see people glancing at her as they walked past; some were smiling and others curious. Looking at herself from their perspective, they would see a smartly dressed but relatively plain elderly woman in conversation with an attractive man wearing a pilot's uniform, who was holding a bunch of red roses.

'Erm, yes, I am Edith. Pleased to meet you,' was all she could say.

'Do you have the money?'

'Yes. It's an awful lot to be carrying around, and I'll be glad to hand it over.'

'That's champion, Edith. As soon as customs have this, then the sheikh will be allowed to leave. He asked me to give you these roses, and also a little something else.' Handing Edith the roses, he then bent his head and leant in towards her, planting a gentle kiss on her lips. Then, turning on his heels, he walked swiftly away, holding the carrier bag tightly in his hand.

Edith was in a daze and touched her lips where the kiss had been planted. She had forgotten to ask what she should do next but assumed that she just had to be patient and wait in the airport.

Two hours later, and she was still waiting. A text to the sheikh and two phone calls went unanswered. Edith went to the information desk to enquire about a private plane landing from the United Arab Emirates. The woman behind the desk looked at Edith. 'Are you sure you've got the correct information, madam?'

'Yes, quite sure. I'm meeting Sheikh Omar El Sharm, who flew in this morning on his private plane, and I was instructed to go to the arrivals hall in South Terminal. He's been held up, though, by customs, although I would have thought he'd have been cleared by now.'

When the woman on the information desk heard the man's name, she gave a little laugh and then covered it up with a cough. Frowning, as she realised there was something very wrong with the situation, she looked at the elderly woman standing on the other side of the counter who was clutching a bunch of red roses. 'I'm sorry, madam, but private planes have their own landing strip and terminal. The person you're meeting would not have come through into the general arrivals hall. Are you sure you're not mistaken?'

Edith felt herself getting flustered. 'Of course I'm not mistaken. And I've just met the pilot, who gave me these flowers.' Edith held them aloft for the woman to see.

'I think I need to call the airport police. There is something not quite right here. If you're happy to wait here, I'll call them now.'

This alarmed Edith, who disliked fuss of any sort. 'No! No, don't do that. I don't want to cause any bother or have any fuss. I'm sorry to have troubled you.' And with that, Edith walked briskly away and headed to the train station to catch the Gatwick Express back to Brighton. *There must be an explanation*, she thought, but her subconscious told her that she was a delusional, silly woman who had just been made a fool of.

Arriving at Brighton Station, she caught the bus back to Woodingdean where she lived. Letting herself into her house, and not even taking her coat off, she went upstairs to the study and switched on her computer. Logging onto the dating website where she had first met Sheikh Omar, she searched for him but his profile had been taken down. She called the first bank she had transferred the first lot of money from and asked if they were able to trace the money if she gave them the recipient's bank details. The young male customer service representative asked her to hold on. What he told her on his return was not what Edith wanted to hear. The money had entered the other person's account and had immediately been transferred to another account with a different bank. 'I can give you the receiving bank's telephone number, if you like,' said the young man. 'Can I also suggest, Miss Bonnington, that you let me transfer you to our fraud department. I don't want to alarm you, but we've seen quite a lot of these kinds of transactions

of late. It's known as "authorised push payment" fraud
and it's on the increase.'

'No, I don't want to do that. It's okay. I need to do a
bit of thinking but thank you.'

'Well, if you're sure. Is there anything else I can help
you with today?'

'No thank you.' She hung up, knowing it would be
pointless to call the other bank as the story would be the
same.

It was then that Edith knew she had been the victim of
a con man, and a very clever one at that. Not only had
she suffered the loss of what was for her a lot of money,
but she had also suffered a loss of face. Losing the
money was bad enough, but how could she ever face
her friends again after this. Margaret's words sprang into
her consciousness… *"But why would a rich Arab sheikh,
who lives in a palace, and has his own plane, be interested
in you?"*

Well, thought Edith, her friend was right this time,
as was her mother, who had often declared, 'Edith, I
sometimes think you live in a dreamworld.'

SUSIE

The money had left Susie's account a while ago, and she had heard nothing from Tim since then. Her emails bounced back with an "unable to deliver" message. She logged onto the dating website, but his profile was no longer there. Susie just couldn't understand it. She carried out a search of his name in America, typing in the keywords "Hollywood" and "Los Angeles" in the search bar. Plenty of actors came up with the name of Tim and Timothy, but not with his surname. She went back onto the Wikipedia website again and noticed that it had been updated to show his recent stint at the theatre, but that was all. There was no mention of screen tests, or trips to the USA. She telephoned the theatre to enquire if the play, after all, had been transferred to the West End or any other theatre. The member of staff told Susie that it had ended its run and would not be transferring anywhere else.

Susie was feeling very concerned and not sure what to do next. It still hadn't occurred to her that things weren't as they should be. That evening, she poured herself a glass of wine and sat down to watch *Vera* on ITV. The advertisements came on, and one showed two men advertising a well-known car rental firm. She couldn't believe what she saw. It was Tim! Tim was one of the salesmen. She made a note of the time the advertisement was shown and decided that, the following day, she would try and track him down. She reassured herself that there must be a legitimate reason why he hadn't contacted her because, after all, she had lent him money. However, she didn't understand why he hadn't told her about his appearance in the advertisement and was puzzled by this. With so many questions swirling about in her head, she found it difficult to concentrate on her favourite TV programme any longer and went to bed, where she had a sleepless night.

The following day was an afternoon shift for Susie, and so she decided to use the morning productively. Making a pot of coffee, she set to work. Whilst she could certainly be accused of being gullible, no one could ever say she was not resilient or tenacious. Her first call was to the head office of the car rental firm whose television advertisement she had seen Tim in. Getting through to the receptionist, she asked to be put through to the department who dealt with advertising.

'That would be our Sales, Marketing, and Advertising Department,' said the receptionist. 'Hold on, and I'll connect you.'

Susie was put through to a member of staff and asked them if they could tell her which advertising agency they used for that particular advert. Susie knew she would probably be asked why she wanted the information, and she had her answer prepared.

'I work for a company who compile a list of advertisements to put forward for the National Television Advertising Awards. Your company's advertisement has been selected, and so we need to know which agency you used.' Susie marvelled at her inventiveness and gave herself a pat on the back. The employee on the other end of the phone asked her to hold on whilst she went and looked up the information in the files.

'Right, the agency we used are called Effective Advertising. Would you like their telephone number, and the person to speak to?'

Susie said she would and thanked the woman for her help. Her next call was to Effective Advertising, where she asked the receptionist to put her through to Chantelle Fleming, who was in charge of casting. A breezy voice said, 'Hello. Chantelle speaking. How may I help you?'

'Hello, Chantelle. My name is Susie Bickerstaff and I'm enquiring about an advertisement I saw the other evening that your company did for Ace Car Rentals. The company I work for would like to use one of the actors who appeared in your commercial, but we don't know how to contact him.' Susie gave the person Tim's name and crossed her fingers.

'Can you hold on whilst I look in the files? Obviously, I can't give you any personal details, if we have any on file that is, but I could let you have his agent's number. Would that be sufficient?'

Susie let out a sigh of relief, as she had expected it to be more difficult. 'Yes please. That would be perfect,' she replied.

When Chantelle gave Susie the name of Tim's agent, she was surprised to see that it wasn't a Mr Mitchelson, as she was absolutely certain that Tim had said his agent was called Mitchelson and she had transferred the money to that person's account. Thanking Chantelle for her help, she then called the number she had been given and spoke to yet another receptionist.

'Hello, can you help me please? I'm trying to track down an actor who is on your books.' Susie gave the receptionist Tim's name.

'What is this in connection with? You know I'm not able to give out personal information over the phone?'

'Yes, I realise that,' said Susie. 'The thing is, it's a bit of a delicate matter. I lent Tim some money so that he could go for a screen test in Los Angeles.'

The receptionist burst out laughing. 'Is this a prank call by any chance?' said the girl.

'No, it most certainly isn't,' replied Susie in an affronted tone. 'Look, can I speak to his agent please? I'm fed up with speaking to receptionists all the time.'

'Well, excuse me!' said the girl. 'Hold on, I'll see if Mr Broadstairs will take your call.'

Susie heard a click on the other end of the phone, and then a booming voice announced, 'Manny Broadstairs. How can I help you? Felicity tells me you're trying to track down Timmo.'

Having finally got to speak to the person in charge, Susie told the agent the full story. When she mentioned the screen test in Los Angeles, Manny Broadstairs chuckled. 'I'm sorry to laugh, but there's no way old Timmo could ever be cast in a Hollywood film. He just doesn't have screen presence, and his acting ability is questionable as well. Although you could say that about a lot of actors these days. To be honest with you, Miss...'

'You can call me Susie.'

'To be honest with you, Susie, it's difficult enough getting him the work he has over here. He only got the part in the advertisement you saw recently, because it didn't require any acting skills and he only had one line to say.'

Susie realised that what the agent had said was true, because all Tim had done was to stand still and utter the words "we're better than the competition".

Manny Broadstairs then asked Susie if she had reported this to the police. She replied that she hadn't, and it had never occurred to her to do so.

'Well, look, m'dear, leave this with me. I'll get in touch with Timmo and get back to you. Can you give me a number to get back to you on, and also the email address you say he contacted you from?

*

A few days passed, and Susie was at a loss as to what had happened. In fact, she was thoroughly bewildered, and found it difficult to concentrate at work and at home. Finally, her mobile rang, and it was the agent. Manny's usual jocular tone when talking about "Timmo" had disappeared and "Timmo" became a sombrely uttered "Tim". 'Firstly, Susie, I can totally vouch for Tim. I've known him for a long time. Since he started out in the acting business, to be accurate. Secondly, and I'm sorry to tell you this, but you have been the victim of a con man and poor old Tim has been the victim of identity theft. That email address you have does not belong to Tim, and never has. He is, quite understandably, upset about this, and will report it to the police. I suggest you do the same. I'm sorry, m'dear, but that's the best I can do.'

Susie knew then what she had been afraid to admit to herself, that she had been conned by a very clever and devious man, posing as a real actor, who had stolen – what was to her – a large amount of money, and which she would probably never see again. When she looked back on the conversations she had conducted with the person who had called himself Tim, she realised that, apart from one solitary phone call, he had never once asked her anything about herself or tried to cheer her up when she'd had a bad day. It had been all one-way, and always all about him.

MITCH

Mitch could feel a tingling of excitement and anticipation, which made him unable to sit still or concentrate. He needed to calm himself down, and so decided to go for a long walk along the seafront. The day was slightly blustery, and he felt the sun and wind on his face which would give him a nice tan, as the fake one had worn off. He had kept the stubble as he felt it made him look trendier and added to his naturally attractive looks. As he walked, he mentally ticked off what he had completed so far, and what he still had to do: Edith; "completed", Susie; "completed", Mrs B; "almost completed", and Fiona; "to do". *Ah, lovely Fiona,* he thought. *I'll be seeing you soon.*

The next morning, as he was leaving for "work", Dorothy caught up with him in the hallway. 'Daniel, I was checking my bank account and I noticed that my cheque hasn't been paid in yet. Is there a problem?'

'No, not at all, Mrs B. It's just that it's such an awful lot of money. Are you sure about this?'

'Of course I am, Daniel. It would make me happy to do this for your son, and I'm sure it will ease things financially for you and your wife. Now, pay that cheque in.'

'Okay, will do. Again, I can't thank you enough for your generosity.'

'Glad to be of help. Have a good day, Daniel. See you later,' said Dorothy, smiling, and went back into her living room.

Today, Mitch was off exploring the county of Surrey. When Project Susie was underway, he had considered visiting Guildford but decided it wasn't necessary. A mischievous part of him, however, would have liked to have seen where she lived and to perhaps have bumped into her. She wouldn't, of course, recognise him and Mitch imagined a scenario where he perhaps chatted her up, and asked her if she had a boyfriend.

Swiftly pushing that thought to one side, he headed on to the M25 and took the Wisley turn off onto the A3. He had looked at the map of Surrey the previous evening and noted down a few place names. He had then searched the property websites and carried out his usual searches. Looking at some of the houses for sale, and the prices being asked, he knew he was in millionaire country. He drove through some of the villages; all of them seemed to have the ubiquitous village pub, store-cum-post office, and cricket club. He finally found himself in a small town called Cornham. Driving through the high street, he noticed that the shops were of the independent variety rather than a chain, and the same with the cafés and restaurants. As for supermarkets, there was not an Aldi, Lidl, or Asda in sight. Only an independently owned small supermarket and delicatessen. Driving a Ford Fiesta, Mitch felt very out of place as most of the cars he saw were Mercedes, Audis, and Range Rovers. He even spotted a sleek black Tesla, a green Aston Martin, and a red Ferrari. Many of the cars also had personalised number plates. He decided that, as soon as he could, he would upgrade his car.

Eventually, he came to a pub in a village on the outskirts of Cornham. Parking his car in the car park, which was also full of luxury vehicles, he walked into a traditional pub with oak beams and solid wood tables and chairs. The pub advertised "Real Ale" and "Good Pub Grub". As it was lunchtime, the pub was busy and clearly a local for office workers, and those who lived nearby. The bar area was dominated by men of retirement age all talking in loud voices. Mitch took in their county "uniform" of striped or checked shirts, with pale pink or pale blue jumpers casually thrown over their shoulders. The look was completed by red or tan-coloured trousers, and all of the men wore loafers or boating shoes. *Why, oh why, oh why, do they have to talk so loudly,* thought Mitch; especially the one who had shouted to a tall, sturdy-looking man standing at the other end of the bar. 'Roly, old boy, how's the handicap?' Mitch, who couldn't see a walking stick, wheelchair, or any sign of a disability, realised that "Mr Loudmouth" was probably referring to golf. *Pratts, all of them,* he thought.

After lunch, he began the drive back to East Sussex. Passing by a hotel which had a spa, and was advertising a weekend "special deal", he parked the car and went in to enquire as to the price of the deal and what it included. Also, if there was any availability. The receptionist informed him that there were a few rooms remaining, and that the package included one night's dinner, bed, and breakfast, and a complimentary bottle of Prosecco. She also informed him that, subject to availability, there was a 10% discount on beauty treatments. The cost of the package was more than he would have liked to pay, but he reasoned that this was for a very good cause and booked it on the spot. 'Can I pay cash?' he had asked. He then went into the beauty salon and enquired at the reception desk if there was any free space for a 30-minute massage, explaining that, 'It's a surprise for my wife. It's our anniversary.'

Looking at her screen, the receptionist replied, 'You're in luck, Mr Simpson, and there's a 10% discount. Would 3 o'clock be suitable?'

'Yes, that's perfect. Thank you. Can I pay you now, in cash, if possible?' And it was all organised.

Mitch arrived back in Saltdean exhausted, but the day's exploration had proved useful as he had drawn inspiration from what he had seen. Having had a substantial lunch of steak and ale pie, crushed potatoes and "greens", all washed down with a large glass of Merlot, he fell into a deep sleep and dreamt that he was driving a racing green Morgan along the Nice coastline.

*

Saturday came and Mitch woke up bright and early. Today he was picking up Fiona and they were going away for the weekend. He had explained to a very tetchy Marnie over the telephone why he had to do this and placated her with lots of promises.

'Well, you'd better keep them, Mitch Mitchelson, otherwise it's curtains for us.'

Yeah, yeah, he thought, *I've heard it all before.* He packed his overnight bag and came out of his room whistling.

'You're in a cheerful mood today, Daniel. Off to see your wife?'

'Yes Mrs B, and I'm taking her away for the weekend to give her a change of scenery.'

'Are you taking wee Danny with you?' enquired Dorothy.

Christ, thought Mitch, *I'd forgotten about "wee Danny". I must be careful.* 'No, Mrs B. The wife's sister has offered to care for him. Very good of her in the circumstances, seeing as they haven't helped us much at all. Well, must go. Cheerio.' And he left with a smile and a wave.

Mitch drove away from Saltdean and headed towards Hove where Fiona lived. Gaining entry into the development, he pressed the buzzer to her apartment. He could hear footsteps coming down the stairs, and then the door opened to reveal Fiona dressed in colours of the Union Jack. She was wearing white trousers, a red t-shirt, and navy-blue cardigan trimmed with white edging. With sunglasses perched on the top of her head, she looked, to Mitch, very sophisticated. She was carrying an overnight bag, which he recognised from the brown and beige colours and the intertwined letters of the brand, as being a very expensive, designer brand. *Bloody hell*, he thought, *I've hit the jackpot!* But he knew that anyway. They embraced and kissed each other on the lips.

'Ooh, you smell nice,' said Fiona.

'And so do you,' replied Mitch, grinning.

After seeing all the posh cars in Cornham, he now felt slightly awkward at picking Fiona up in his Ford Fiesta and wished it was something a bit flashier. However, when they had gone out to dinner, she hadn't seemed to notice, and he realised she probably wasn't into cars that much, seeing as she didn't even own one and managed to get around using the excellent bus and train service that served the Brighton area.

'I'm excited. Where are we going?' she asked.

'A trip in the country,' he replied, turning to smile at her.

'Was your son okay with not seeing you this weekend?' she asked.

'He was naturally disappointed, but I promised that I would take a day off in the week and see him then. I had to grovel to the ex, of course, but she agreed as long as I collected him from school and took him out for a pizza. Do you know what she said then? She said, "He'd like that. He'd feel as if he had a real dad again". Bloody cheek of the woman. I've always been a real dad. Honestly, she can be a right b—' Mitch never finished the word because he could feel himself getting carried away with the story and becoming genuinely angry. *I'd be a good method actor; much better than that Tim*, he thought to himself. Also, he was aware that Fiona had gone very quiet. 'Sorry, Fiona. I didn't mean to rant like that. I don't want anything to spoil our weekend. It's just so difficult sometimes.'

'It's all right, Dan. Rant away, if it makes you feel better.'

They drove along in silence for a while, and then Mitch had a worrying thought. Fiona had never said where she lived during her marriage. He knew her husband was wealthy, and therefore assumed they had lived in a wealthy area. It crossed his mind perhaps she had lived in the very area of Surrey where he was now taking her. He began to perspire slightly, as he knew he must ask her where she had lived previously. He could kick himself for not having thought of this before. In what he hoped was a nonchalant tone, he asked, 'Tell me, Fiona, where did you used to live when you were married? I don't think you've ever told me.'

'No, I haven't, have I? That's because I've left it all behind. Anyway, it was Sandbanks, which is near Bournemouth. Very exclusive, I suppose, because you had to have a certain level of income to own a property there, which excluded most people. A bit like the area we're driving through actually, if the houses are anything to go by, except, of course, we're in the country and not by the sea. The one good thing about Sandbanks was that it had a beautiful beach, and I knew when I left that I would always want to live by the sea.'

Mitch let out a sigh of relief. He had never been to Bournemouth, and he had never heard of Sandbanks. *Thank you, God*, he said to himself, and quickly raised his eyes upwards.

Finally, they arrived at the hotel, which Fiona exclaimed looked very nice. Collecting the keys to their room, they caught the lift up. Once in the room, they kissed and then went to bed.

There was, without doubt, sexual chemistry between them, which made Mitch's life easier and, of course, pleasurable. He couldn't describe Fiona as imaginative in bed, or experimental on the sexual side, but she knew what moves to make and her suppleness allowed for deep penetration. *Christ, I have a hard life*, he thought, and then laughed at his cleverness with words.

'What are you laughing at, Dan? What's tickled you so much?' asked Fiona, grinning.

'You have, Fiona. You've tickled me.' They both laughed in unison. 'Crikey, have you seen the time? Right, I've booked you a massage at 3 o'clock in the beauty salon. You'd better get down their now.'

'Oh, what a nice surprise! Thank you. What will you do whilst I'm away?'

'I'm having a rest. You've tired me out with your demands. You're insatiable. Now, run along.' Mitch leapt up to smack her on the bottom.

'I'm going. I'm going,' she said gleefully.

'A minute ago, you were saying, "I'm coming. I'm coming".'

'Daniel Simpson, you're a very naughty man. See you later.' Fiona blew him a kiss and left.

Whilst Fiona was having her 30-minute massage, Mitch asked for the free bottle of Prosecco to be brought up. Feeling guilty that he was having a good time with a woman other than his wife, he decided to call Marnie.

'Marnie, it's me. How are you?' he asked.

'How do you think I am? I'm stuck here, and you're in some posh hotel down south. Just what are you getting up to, Mitch?'

'That, Marnie, is for me to know and for you not to know.' Mitch could hear the key in the door, which alerted him that Fiona was back. Before Marnie could respond, Mitch said 'Got to go, Marnie. Catch you later.' And he hung up.

Fiona came into the room. 'Dan, for some reason the staff called me Mrs Simpson, and wished me a happy anniversary. What's... Oh, how nice. You've ordered a bottle of bubbly. What's the occasion?'

'Sit down, Fiona. I've got something to ask you.'

Getting down on one knee, Mitch put his hand in his dressing gown pocket and pulled out a small blue box. Opening it up, he took out the engagement ring that Marnie had once worn and put it on Fiona's finger. 'Fiona, darling, will you marry me?'

Taken completely by surprise, Fiona responded with, 'Oh my gosh! I don't know what to say. This has come as a total surprise. We haven't even known each other that long.'

'I know, it's incredible, isn't it? Meeting you has been like a bolt out of the blue. I've never ever felt this way before. Say yes, Fiona. Just say yes.' Mitch looked imploringly at Fiona, wishing she would hurry up as his knee was beginning to ache.

'Get up, Dan. You look as if you're uncomfortable.'

Mitch stood up and stretched his legs. He noticed that the ring was a bit loose on Fiona's finger. 'The ring belonged to my mother, and she was on the plump side. I can get it made smaller. Just say the word.'

'How come your wife didn't have this ring?' asked Fiona, looking puzzled.

Mitch was aware that things weren't going as smoothly as he hoped, but he was clever and had answers for everything. 'Well, it's like this. My mother, God rest her soul, never liked my choice of wife. She gave me this ring just before she died, and said "My dear Daniel, this ring was my mother's engagement ring. Keep it safe until you meet the right woman to give it to". But, Mother, I said, I'm married to Mavis and she's got a ring. "She's not the right woman for you, Daniel. That's why I didn't give you the ring when you told me you were proposing to her. You'll know when you meet the right one", and then she died, Fiona. Just like that, she was gone, but I've held onto the ring and never forgot her words. So, Fiona, darling, will you marry me?'

'Yes, I will, Dan. I will marry you,' said Fiona, who felt that it would be very unkind to turn him down. 'On one condition, though.'

'Oh, and what's that then?' said Mitch, slightly truculently.

'That we have a long engagement so that we can get to know each other a bit more. After all, there's no rush as we've got the rest of our lives together.'

Mitch let out a big sigh. 'I thought, for a moment, you were going to say no. What a relief. Yes, then, to a long engagement. Let's celebrate with a glass of Prosecco, and then shall we go to bed, before we have to get ready for dinner?' he asked with a big grin.

Sunday morning came, and after breakfast they had a leisurely drive back to Hove. Mitch dropped Fiona off, with a promise that he would come back later. She had put him off though. 'Don't be offended, Dan, but this has all come as a bit of a surprise, and I need to process it all. How about you come by tomorrow evening?'

Although slightly taken aback by Fiona's response, Mitch played it cool. Shrugging his shoulders, he said, 'Tomorrow is great. We could go out for dinner locally if you want.'

'We're engaged now, Dan, and we've just been away, so I'll cook us dinner. My cooking is an acquired taste, so the sooner you're introduced to it, the less of a shock it will be.' And she laughed happily.

Fiona let herself into her apartment and reflected on the past day's events. In a short space of time, she had gone from being a divorced single woman, to being engaged to a man she had only known for a short while and who she knew hardly anything about. *It's all a bit quick*, she thought, *but he's good-looking, charming, thoughtful, and has restored my confidence.* Fiona's ex-husband, who had never complimented her, and only ever criticised things she did, had made her confidence and self-esteem dwindle little by little until she could no longer bear to look at herself in the mirror at home, or in shops, because she didn't like what she saw. She had undergone counselling for mild body dysmorphia and had finally been made to realise that the problem lay with her husband, rather than her. Thus, she went to bed that night and relived the weekend, falling asleep with a smile on her face.

After the meal on Monday evening, Fiona asked Dan if he was staying over and was surprised when he said no.

'The thing is, Fiona, my landlady is being a bit difficult. I'm not sure why, as I made it clear from the outset that I would only need lodgings from Monday to Friday, and that as I work on contract and divide my time between Shoreham and Newhaven, that I wasn't a nine-to-fiver and so would come and go at different times. She was perfectly fine with that, and then you wouldn't believe it. She said to me the other day, "Mr Simpson, can I have a word please. I don't know where I am with you. Coming and going all the time. I never know if you're in or out". I was flabbergasted, Fiona. Really, I was!'

Before Fiona could respond, he had continued, 'And what annoyed me further, especially as I always pay my rent on time, is when she said, "Oh, and by the way, Mr Simpson, you didn't pay for the Friday night you stayed". I said to her, what Friday night is that, Mrs Baxter? And do you know what she said? She said, "The Friday night you stayed over before you went away for the weekend". Well, I can tell you, I could feel myself getting annoyed, so I just walked away. However, I feel I should show my face tonight, as I don't want to incur her wrath again. She's quite a formidable woman. Oh, and I also promised Danny I would go up and see him this week.'

'Well, that explains things then,' said Fiona, having managed at last to get a word in. 'When will I see you next?'

'I'll ring you,' he had casually replied, before briefly kissing her on cheek and leaving.

One thing Mitch was good at was thinking on his feet. He had almost let slip Dorothy's surname and then realised that Fiona might take it upon herself at some later date to try and track down a Mrs Beresford. So, he had given the false name of Baxter.

*

The denouement was coming, and Mitch drove up to see Marnie in Luton where he would spend the next few days, getting the final pieces of the jigsaw in place. This was the most difficult part, and timing was crucial. Nearly a week had gone by, during which time Mitch was attentive and affectionate towards Marnie. Sexually, she was strictly "vanilla", as was Fiona, but Marnie had none of the suppleness and wriggly moves that Fiona had. *If truth be told*, thought Mitch, *having sex with Marnie was like humping an inanimate object*. However, he needed her on board and she really was a docile and accommodating wife, who was grateful for any crumbs of affection he threw her way.

It was time to call Fiona. 'Hi Fiona, it's Dan. Sorry I haven't called sooner, but I wanted to give some quality time to Danny and explain to him how I've met a lovely lady to whom I'm now engaged, and that he would still be a part of my new life down South. I hope you didn't mind my telling him that he could stay with us whenever he wanted to, as long as his mum agreed.'

Fiona wished that Dan had discussed this with her first but could hardly refuse, so she simply replied, 'He will always be welcome, Dan. I can't wait to meet him.'

Then he had dropped a bombshell. 'I've got a problem, Fiona. As I was leaving my lodgings to make the trip up to see Danny, I explained to Mrs Baxter that I would be gone for a few days. Do you know what she said? She said, "I think it's best, Mr Simpson, if we terminate our arrangement. Don't you agree?". Well, I was going to reply, "No I don't agree", but it's for the best, I suppose. The thing is, Fiona, I don't have anywhere to stay when I come back down. Can I stay with you until I find new lodgings?'

Without hesitation, she had replied, 'Don't be silly, Dan. We're engaged to be married. You can move in with me. It makes perfect sense to do so.'

All the pieces fell into place. Mitch had gone back to see Dorothy and explained that they were finalising the arrangements to travel to the States with Danny, and, regrettably, he was giving notice. She had replied that she was sorry to see him go but was glad of the assistance she'd been able to provide and asked that he kept in touch. Mitch packed his belongings and moved in with Fiona.

DOROTHY

A few weeks had passed by and Dorothy had heard nothing from Daniel, apart from a letter written in what looked like a child's handwriting: *Dear Aunty Dorothy, Thank you for saving my life, and for making my mum and dad happy again. Lots of love "wee Danny" xxx* There was no address on the letter, and so Dorothy was unable to reply. More weeks went by, and still no news. It was whilst she was having her morning cup of coffee, that she realised a number of things about her lodger. She had never had an address for him; she didn't know exactly what job he did and, more importantly, she had never had a reply to her requests for references and had forgotten to follow them up. The money had left her account, at her insistence, she now realised, and so she was puzzled. It occurred to her at that very moment that she had been tricked by a con man, albeit a very personable and convincing one.

*

Dorothy's life continued and she still had her weekly Wednesday coffee mornings with her friends from the Church. However, she had never told them that she had lent her lodger money. It was at one of those meetings that one of them had asked, 'How's your lodger, Dorothy? You don't talk about him as much as you used to.'

Dorothy had replied, 'Oh, he left a while ago. And before you ask, no, I won't bother getting another one. I'll get myself a dog instead. They're less trouble, aren't they Bobo?' She gave Bobo a pat on the head.

'Woof', said Bobo in response.

FIONA

Life was blissful living with Dan. He went off to work every morning; sometimes Shoreham or Newhaven, and Fiona continued with her voluntary work. She had asked the charity if she could work in the Brighton shop, rather than travelling to Worthing, and the charity had agreed. Every evening, over a glass of wine, they would share stories of each other's day, watch some television, and then go to bed and make love. Sometimes they would go out for a drink and a meal, but they were quite happy just being in each other's company. It was like existing in a bubble of cosy coupledom, something she had never experienced with her ex-husband. And then, one day, there was a phone call and Dan announced that he had to make an urgent trip back up north.

'Oh dear, I hope it's nothing too serious,' Fiona had said. 'When will you be back?'

'I'm not sure. Don't worry, I'll keep you posted,' he had replied, and packed his bag and suddenly left.

*

A few days later, Fiona arrived back from her shift as a volunteer to find Dan, who had not contacted her at all whilst he had been away, sitting in the chair with his head in his hands.

'Whatever is the matter, Dan?' she had asked. 'You look awful. What's happened? It's not Danny, is it?'

'Dan had looked up at her with a glum face. 'It is to do with Danny, although nothing serious like an illness or accident. It's my ex. She's got me well and truly over a barrel.'

Fiona had sat down on the settee. 'You'd better tell me the whole story. You'll feel better for getting it off your chest.'

Dan had got up from the chair and went to sit on the settee with Fiona. Holding her hands in his, he looked at her sadly. 'Not surprisingly, my ex isn't happy I've found someone I want to be with for the rest of my life. There are things I haven't told you, my love.' He let go of Fiona's hands and rested his palms on his knees.

'Mavis still lives in the family home with Danny that we bought together with a joint mortgage. When I moved out, at her insistence, I should add, I purchased a one-bedroom flat to live in which I will, of course, sell. I have still been paying my share of the mortgage, and also giving her maintenance for Danny which I am legally obliged to do, and, of course, I wouldn't dream of not supporting him. She was supposed to pay her share of the mortgage, and all the bills because, after all, she is living there. Anyway, the silly bitch – sorry, Fiona, I shouldn't have said that – has not been keeping up the mortgage payments, and has also got behind with the bills, and now the bank has sent a letter to say that, unless the mortgage arrears are cleared, the property will be repossessed. It's not enough that I've been paying my share. So, she's got me over a barrel. She's said that I've got to clear the arrears and take on the full mortgage, and if I don't, she won't let me see Danny.'

Fiona was shocked to hear all of this. 'I don't think she can do that, Dan,' she had said. 'You're Danny's father, and you have every right to see your son.'

'You don't know her, Fiona. She's a horrid woman who will do anything she can to get back at me. Anyway, so I agreed – stupid person that I am – to take on the full mortgage. But I said to her, that means ownership of the house has to then be transferred to me, and then I can sell it. I'm not an unreasonable man, Fiona. Very reasonably, and generously, if I may say so, I said I would, of course, give her some of the sale proceeds so that she could buy herself a smaller place for her and Danny to live in. Do you know what she said? She said, "Oh no you don't. The house is mine and Danny's until such time as he no longer wants to live here, and then I'll live here for as long as I want". And then it was the usual blah, blah, blah, "You've taken the best years of my life, and now you're swanning around with your..." And I can't repeat the word she called you, Fiona. Anyway, the long and the short of it is this. I have two options. I can either go back up north and live in my one-bedroom flat so that I get to maintain contact with my son, or I give her £60,000 to clear the mortgage debt and bills, and she also gets to keep the house, which is what she really wants. If I do that, she has promised that I can still have access to Danny whenever I want.'

'What a mess, Dan. It seems very unfair to me. Also, if you have to go back up north for the foreseeable future, where does that leave us? I love you, Dan, I really do, but I don't want to move away from here.'

'We're in a bit of pickle, aren't we? I can't see a way out.'

Fiona had listened to all of this with dismay. Her newfound feelings of happiness had vanished in an instant. She came to a decision. 'I think I have a solution, Dan. I could lend you the £60,000, and then once you sell your flat you can repay me. How does that sound?'

'I couldn't possibly accept, Fiona. That's no way to start married life, with your new husband owing you money.'

'There's no other way, Dan. You could try and get a bank loan, I suppose, but think of the interest you'd have to pay. I can let you have the money. That's not a problem. Then you can clear the debts, and Danny can come and see us whenever he wants. I do think, though, Dan, that you should get a solicitor's letter drawn up so that she can't come back for more money, or renege on your verbal agreement.

'She wouldn't like that, Fiona. It may cause further problems if I do that.'

'Oh well, it's up to you, I suppose.' She shrugged her shoulders.

'Well, if you're sure about the offer, Fiona, I'll take you up on it. Danny is the only good thing to have come out of my disastrous marriage. My old mother was right – I married the wrong woman, and now I'm marrying the right one.'

Fiona smiled, but inside she felt a bit deflated and a feeling rose up in her that something had been lost, and the relationship was no longer as perfect as it had been. Looking at Dan, and sighing, she said, 'That's settled then. Shall I do a bank transfer to your account?'

'No, it's best you do it directly to her account to keep her off my back. It's in the name of M. Simpson.'

Fiona frowned. 'Are you sure that's the right thing to do, Dan? She might hang onto the money, rather than clear the debts.'

'Don't worry, Fiona. I'll make sure she uses the money as it should be used.'

*

A week later, Fiona came home and went into the bedroom to change out of her work clothes. She was struck by the silence. This was not unusual, of course, but today she sensed an atmosphere of absence. Dan usually left some item of clothing on the chair, or socks on the floor, but there was nothing of his lying around. She opened the wardrobe, and all of his clothes had gone. Similarly, with the two drawers she had given him, both were empty. She went into the bathroom and noticed that all his toiletries were gone. Her intuition kicked in, and she went to her jewellery box on the dressing table. She went to the compartment where she kept her earrings and noticed that the ones Dan had bought her, with green tassels, were missing. Fiona had a sudden sinking feeling in the pit of her stomach, as if she had been punched. She went into the living room and saw a piece of paper on the coffee table. It had one word written on it: "SORRY".

She had transferred the sum of £60,000 from two of her bank accounts, even though both banks had precautionary alerts in place advising people to act with care when transferring money. She would, of course, report it to the police, but knew there was probably very little that could be done. Fiona realised that she had fallen for a charming and thoroughly likeable con man. She would also try and track down the landlady, Mrs Baxter, but didn't hold out much hope on that either.

*

A month later, Fiona took a walk along the seafront and headed for Brighton Pier. Walking to the very end of the pier, she took off the loose engagement ring and tossed it into the sea. If she could take anything positive out of the experience, it was this: she knew, in her heart, that Dan (if that was his real name, which she doubted) had genuinely found her attractive and sexually desirable. There were some things that couldn't be faked. It also struck her that he had never said to her "I love you". Shrugging her shoulders, she made her way back to Hove and decided to stay single for the time being.

MITCH AND MARNIE

Mitch had arrived back in Luton and rushed up the stairs, startling Marnie when he had burst in through the door and shouted, 'Right Marnie, get packing.'

'Where are we going?' she asked.

'We're going up in the world,' he replied.

PART THREE

MITCH AND MARNIE

The first thing Mitch did before he and Marnie moved to Surrey was to upgrade his Ford Fiesta. He knew he wouldn't get much for it, but any trade-in value was better than nothing. Having conducted initial research on the internet, he found a car leasing company that had a good selection of cars, with a variety of leasing arrangements. He found a red Mercedes-Benz A200 sport, with four doors and an automatic gearbox. The money he would get for his Ford would pay for the initial deposit, and then he could lease it on a 48-month contract for £254 a month. In any event, Mitch had no intention of keeping the car for that long, and so could easily afford the monthly payment. He always had a bit of a wobble when he had to provide information for credit reference purposes, but somehow always managed to get through the checks. Car leasing had become very popular, as it provided a way for people who couldn't afford to buy flash or luxury cars outright and by leasing them, it at least gave the impression of wealth. So, Mitch reasoned that even if there was a problem with a financial check, it probably would be overlooked as the salespeople would hardly turn business away.

The second thing Mitch did was a bit trickier to organise. On his earlier foray around Surrey, he had discovered a very upmarket road near to the pub where he had stopped to have lunch. Nearby was an estate which was gated at both ends, surrounded by high bushes, behind which could be glimpsed a number of large houses. The estate was called Greenwood Park

Estate, and the message was clear: KEEP OUT AND CLEAR OFF. It made Mitch laugh because even though Greenwood Park was called an estate, it was nothing like the estate near to where he grew up. In those estates, you didn't need telling to keep out, because you wouldn't want to go in and, if you did inadvertently stray into it, you cleared off as soon as you could.

Running parallel to the estate was a long tree-lined road, and it was here that he wanted to be for his next "project". He had driven up and down the road a few times to get a feel of the place. One end of the road – and the wrong end for Mitch's purpose – consisted of a care home, doctor's surgery, primary school, and village hall. The middle to top end of the road consisted of large, detached houses built on spacious plots, and nearly all behind gates, some of which had entry systems. The houses spoke of wealthy individuals, as did the cars parked in the driveways. He even spotted a Rolls Royce, although it looked to be ancient.

Mitch had not seen any "For Rent" boards but he knew that in exclusive areas like this, advertising that a house was empty was foolish even if they had alarm systems. So, he went onto his favourite property website, and searched for properties to rent in that specific area. He found two: one was completely out of his budget and, in any case, was far too big; the other was a slightly smaller house on the corner of the road he was interested in. The details on the website stated that it was available for six months, which suited Mitch. In his opinion, the house was still on the large size for two people but probably, in this kind of area, he thought, size did matter. The rent was also high, as to be expected, but manageable, thanks to Fiona. Of course, she wasn't aware that she would be helping Mitch and Marnie pay their rent. She, no doubt, had now password-protected her computer login information, but she didn't know that Mitch had kept a record of all her bank details, account password and memorable information. He would siphon off money from her savings account, and then top up the rest of the rental fee with his own money. If she had checked her accounts recently, no odd withdrawals or payments would have shown up because Mitch hadn't, as yet, taken any money. Therefore, he was guessing that she probably would go back to the habit of not checking her accounts on a regular basis, which had been a previous practice of hers.

He went into the local estate agent and enquired about the property. 'Six months is perfect,' he had said. 'We're relocating back to the UK from Dubai and haven't yet decided exactly where to move to. We like this area, but want to try before we buy,' he had added with a smile.

The agent gave Mitch the usual spiel. 'Oh, I'm sure you and your wife will love this area. Cornham has some lovely shops and restaurants, and there's a good train service into London. When you decide to buy, please do come and see me. It would be a pleasure to help you.'

Blah, blah, blah, thought Mitch, but actually replied, 'Of course. Absolutely. No problem.'

Mitch signed the rental agreement in his late father's name, Clifford. He also completed the direct debit form in which he gave the bank details of a still active account in the name of Clifford Mitchelson, which he had kept open even though his father had long since passed away. Once this current project was completed, he would then close that account for good. The agent enquired about getting references, and Mitch gave two fictitious company names but with real addresses in Dubai that he had found on the internet. The agent raised his eyebrows.

'I can give you the telephone numbers if you prefer? It might be quicker.' Mitch began to fumble in his pocket for his mobile phone.

'No, no, don't worry. We'll send out our standard reference letter. I'm sure we'll get a reply at some point.'

Mitch was relieved. He was betting on the fact that either the letters would be thrown away by the genuine companies listed at the addresses or, by the time a reply was received back to say that there was no company of that name at either address, both he and Marnie would be long gone. The agent had expressed surprise that Mitch hadn't wanted to view the house. 'There's no need,' he had replied, 'the location is perfect, it looks very well maintained from the outside, and I'm sure it's very nice inside. Let's just say my wife and I are taking a leap of faith. If there are any issues, I assume, of course, that you will sort them out?'

'Oh, rest assured, Mr Mitchelson. We have a very good management and maintenance team. Any problems, just give us a ring.' And he handed over the keys.

*

Mitch had picked Marnie up in the new car, which she was delighted with, and then dangled some keys at her.

'What are these?' she said.

'These, Marnie my sweet, are keys to our new home.'

'Is it big?'

'Very big, Marnie,' Mitch replied with a cheeky grin.

'Mitch Mitchelson, you really are a one,' replied Marnie, grinning.

Mitch could tell she was happy, though, and that was half the battle. *Happy wife, happy life*, he thought, and off they drove in the red Mercedes.

*

As Mitch had predicted, the house was perfect. Marnie had moaned because the interior was slightly outdated, and there was no swimming pool or tennis court. However, seeing as she neither played tennis nor shown any interest in swimming for as long as he had known her, he just let the moaning go over his head. If he was honest, he too would have liked an ultra-modern interior; clean lines, cool, almost monochromatic, colours, granite worktops and pale wood flooring throughout. Instead, the interior had a faded elegance which was probably once considered chic. With dark beige fitted carpets, flowery chintz curtains with frills and tie-backs, the rooms were still a lot posher and smarter than anything he and Marnie had ever lived in before. When they walked into the kitchen, Marnie had actually squealed; something she hadn't done in a long while. What had caused this outburst of excitement was the appearance of a double oven.

'Oh, Mitch, a double oven! Think of all the things I can cook,' she had said.

'Does this mean real home cooked food and not ready-prepared convenience food?'

'Of course it does. I'll have to buy some cookery books though.'

Mitch raised his eyes to the ceiling. There was another squeal. Marnie had gone over to the large fridge-freezer and pressed a button on the outside of the fridge. Two lumps of ice had shot out and landed on the floor. 'Mitch, come and look at this. We can get ice from the fridge if we press this button. Also,' and she took a glass from the cupboard and placed it in the compartment next to the ice button and pressed another button, 'cold water. How amazing is that. No more plastic ice trays for us! Oh, Mitch, I just love this house.' She came over and gave him a hug and a peck on the lips.

The reason why the house was perfect for Mitch was due to the fact that it was on the corner of two roads and, from one of the back bedrooms, he had a clear view of the road he was interested in. He had purchased a good pair of binoculars and would use the bedroom, which would also double up as his study, to see the "comings and goings" of the Green Park Road residents on a daily basis and make a chart of their routines. This information would be used for his next project – the big one.

*

Mitch and Marnie spent the next few days familiarising themselves with the area they had moved to. If they had to describe themselves at this particular moment in time, it would be "fishes out of water". It was as if they were inhabiting an alien planet, and they were definitely out of their comfort zone. Whilst Mitch could put on a good act, and appear nonchalant and undaunted by new experiences, Marnie could not. She had steadfastly refused to go into any of the shops in Cornham. They had stood outside one designer boutique with Mitch encouraging Marnie to go inside and have a look round.

'Just go in, and if they ask if you need any help, all you have to say is "No thank you. I'm just looking".'

'There's no way I'm going in, even if you offer to come in with me. The clothes in the window don't even have price tags on. I read somewhere that if you have to ask the price of something, then you can't afford it. Anyway, I bet the women will be horribly snotty.'

She's got a point, I suppose, he thought and was quietly relieved because it might have proved very expensive for him if she had seen something she liked. The next shop Marnie refused to go into was the supermarket-cum-delicatessen.

'But, Marnie,' Mitch remonstrated, 'we need to get stocked up with groceries.'

'Well, I'm not going in there. Look at the window display. There's not one item of food on display I recognise. What's all those little white balls and greasy looking red things in those dishes? And look at the label on that loaf of bread – *Rustic hand-crafted seeded bread with goats cheese and olive stuffing*. What's wrong with good old white sliced bread? I ask you, I don't know what—'

'Okay, Marnie. I see where you're coming from. Just calm down a bit.' Mitch had to admit, some of the food did look a little unappetising, but he and Marnie had never been very adventurous in terms of what they ate. Another thing he noticed was that the prices were very high, and so, in a way, he was relieved when she suggested they have a drive around and find a more ordinary supermarket to do their shopping.

A few days later, they had not long sat down to an early dinner when the doorbell rang. Mitch opened the door to be greeted by a naturally attractive woman. 'Good evening. Sorry to disturb you. I'm Abigail Thomas and I live at number 10, just around the corner from you. I'm your neighbourhood welcome representative.' She extended her hand to Mitch to shake. 'Whenever anyone new moves into the immediate area, the agent alerts us so that we can welcome you and see if you need assistance with anything. Like, for example, doctor surgeries – ours is at the end of the road, by the way – dentists, schools and so on, especially if you're relocating from abroad.'

Yeah right, thought Mitch cynically, *it's to see if we will fit in, more like*. Instead, he replied, 'Well, that's a very neighbourly thing to do. Thank you. Come in and meet Marnie.'

'Marnie, this is Abigail. She's a neighbour come to welcome us to the area.' Marnie stood up. *Please don't curtsey, Marnie,* he silently pleaded.

Marnie did a little dip and put on what she thought was a posh accent. 'How nice to meet you.' She extended her hand to Abigail.

Abigail smiled. 'It's very daunting moving somewhere new, so if I can be of any help whatsoever, call me. I should also add that, at this end of the road, we try and foster a community spirit. We do this by taking it in turns to host a get-together where we have drinks and nibbles and socialise. We all lead busy lives and so it's a nice way of catching up with each other. We also try and come up with ideas for making our road a better place to live. For example, we arranged for speed limit signs to be put up because people were using the road as a cut-through and speeding. We approached the council about this because there's a care home at the other end, and a primary school. The council were useless, so we all clubbed together, purchased the signs, and put them up ourselves. The village hall was also threatened with closure due to lack of use, so myself and the other wives found a couple of instructors and we now run Zumba and yoga classes.' Abigail looked at Marnie and smiled. 'You might like to try these classes and that way you'll meet some of the other wives. So, apart from fostering good neighbourly relationships, we also aim to do some good. Well, I think I've gabbled on too long and taken up your evening. I'll bid you goodbye. No need to show me out.'

When Abigail had left, Mitch and Marnie looked at each other and shrugged. 'What do you think, Mitch?'

'She seems nice enough. Talks too much but seemed very helpful. I'm sure we'll find out in due course what they're all like. Now, our dinner will be cold. Pop it in the microwave, Marnie.'

*

A few weeks passed by in which Mitch and Marnie deliberately kept a low profile. Marnie was happy being a housewife, keeping the house spotlessly clean, cooking simple one-pot meals in the top oven, still not having got to grips with using two ovens, and generally enjoying living in a well-equipped, comfortable and spacious house. In fact, Mitch had never seen her so happy and relaxed. He, on the other hand, was keeping watch on a daily basis of his neighbours' movements and his chart was beginning to take shape. Not having met any of them yet, apart from Abigail, and not knowing their names, he could only put the house numbers on his chart and place faces to the houses. There was one person, however, who did look vaguely familiar and it was obvious to Mitch that this person was up to something. He would find out what later.

The opportunity to meet the rest of their immediate neighbours finally happened. Not expecting to find anything in their post box apart from flyers and other junk mail, Mitch found a white envelope addressed to Mr and Mrs Cliff Mitchelson". Inside was a white card on which were written the words: '*You are cordially invited to our neighbourhood get-together. Friday, 17*th*, 7.30 p.m. Hosts: Rufus and Juliana.*'

Friday came and Marnie was in one of her flaps. 'What on earth am I going to wear, Mitch? I haven't got anything remotely suitable.'

'How do you know you haven't got anything suitable? You haven't met any of the women yet, apart from Abigail, and she was dressed in jeans and a jumper.'

'I've seen a couple of the women. One of them was dressed to the nines and she was just putting a bin out, and the other one I saw coming out of her house in running gear which consisted of pink top, black shorts that were very short, pink socks, and black trainers with pink laces. Oh, and she was wearing pink lipstick. That's how I know I haven't got anything suitable, Mitch.'

Mitch could see Marnie was close to tears. It was definitely much easier being a man when it came to clothes; a pair of chinos, shirt and loafers sufficed for almost anywhere, and you only had to add a tie and a jacket for somewhere a bit more formal. For women, the small matter of clothing and accessories could be highly competitive and judgemental. 'I don't have time to take you shopping today, Marnie. For now, wear that flowered dress I bought you in Luton, and then we'll go on a shopping spree and I'll buy you some new things. Okay?'

Marnie looked slightly pacified. 'I suppose so.'

'Oh, and, Marnie, put a bit of make-up on. Just some mascara and lipstick will do.' Mitch actually felt sorry for Marnie. He had a premonition that he was taking her into the lioness's den. He wasn't proved wrong.

The invitation didn't give the house number for Rufus and Juliana's house, and so Mitch and Marnie casually strolled along the road and waited until they saw people entering what appeared to be the largest house in the road. Of an older, more traditional, design, it stood out in contrast to some of the newer houses at the top end of the road. Mitch and Marnie walked up the gravel driveway behind another couple. On the threshold of the open doorway stood a couple with a commanding presence, who Mitch assumed were their hosts, Rufus and Juliana. Handshakes, "hello, old boy", air kisses on cheeks, and "you look fabulous, darling", greeted the couple in front of Mitch and Marnie. Close up, Mitch recognised Rufus as being "Mr Loudmouth" from the pub, who was also the man whose Wednesday routine needed investigating. Finally, the hosts turned their attention to Mitch (who Rufus knew as Cliff) and Marnie. 'Ah, you must be the Mitchelsons,' said Rufus. 'Come in, then, and we'll introduce you to the rest of the gang.'

Mitch and Marnie entered a cavernous hallway that reminded Mitch of a stately home they had once visited on a day out. Mitch could see that Marnie's eyes and mouth were wide open in amazement, and he nudged her in the ribs. Sensing that she was nervous, he took hold of her hand and was rewarded with a loving smile. Rufus led the way, with Juliana following on behind. They entered a large living room and stood next to Rufus and Juliana in the centre of the room, as if they were on display.

Rufus cleared his throat as a way of getting everyone's attention. 'Listen up, all. We have two new guests with us tonight.' All eyes turned towards the couple they would come to know as Cliff and Marnie. 'Let's give a warm welcome to Mr and Mrs Cliff and Marnie Mitchelson.' Two couples, who looked identical in terms of looks and what they were wearing, smiled and clapped, whilst another couple merely nodded. Abigail smiled and gave a wave, whilst the man sat next to her, which Mitch and Marnie assumed was her husband, gave a slight smile.

Juliana rang a bell that was on one of the side tables, and two young girls came into the room. One was carrying a tray with glasses of red and white wine, and the other was carrying a tray with finger food which, to Mitch and Marnie's eyes, looked very much like the little dishes they had seen in the window of the delicatessen. 'Ah,' said Juliana, 'here's my two lovely grandchildren, India and Chyna. Girls, hand round the nibbles and drinks please.' It was on the tip of Mitch's tongue to ask if their mother was called Brazil but decided against it.

Mitch and Marnie went and sat on one of the large settees, and Mitch took this moment to quickly assess their new neighbours. The blond couple, who had merely nodded, had been introduced as Sven and Svetlana, and were the couple in front of Mitch and Marnie at the entrance. Looking discreetly at Svetlana, he had to admit that she had a nice figure. Dressed in a figure-hugging pale pink dress which clearly showed off her toned body, she had accessorised her outfit with chunky gold jewellery, and strappy pink stiletto shoes. Her carefully applied make-up continued the pink theme. Bright pink lip gloss drew attention to her plump lips, whilst her high cheekbones were enhanced with a shimmery pink blusher. Her white-blond hair was pulled back into a very tight ponytail, giving her blue eyes an exotic slant. She certainly gave off an air of sex appeal and an aura of self-possession, and an alliteration sprang into Mitch's mind of Barbie-blond, big boobs, and bling. In comparison, her husband was pleasant-looking and dressed conservatively in a grey suit, white shirt and pale blue tie. Mitch noticed that his black lace-up shoes had a high sheen to them. Mitch thought that perhaps he had just come from the office.

Rufus, who seemed to be a natural leader, was dressed in exactly the same clothes he had been wearing when Mitch saw him in the pub. His wife, Juliana, was obviously expensively dressed and a bit over the top for what was a casual get-together. Her outfit consisted of black leather trousers, and a jacket with a leopard print design and frills at the neckline and at the end of the sleeves. Whether she wore anything under the jacket, Mitch couldn't tell, but he suspected not because her cleavage was proudly on show. If Marnie wore too little make-up, then Juliana wore far too much, and he suspected that she too, like Svetlana, had indulged in Botox and lip fillers. Her auburn hair was elaborately piled up on the top of her head and looked as if it was about to topple at any moment.

As for Abigail and her husband, Andrew, there was nothing showy about either of them and they sat quietly together sipping their drinks. The two identical couples who had smiled and clapped, were talking animatedly amongst themselves. They had been introduced as Tommy and Tammy, and Toby and Trixie, and Mitch found it difficult to tell them apart, before it dawned on him that he was looking at two sets of identical twins. The twin brothers had married twin sisters. *Well, I never,* thought Mitch, *you couldn't make it up.*

Gradually they all migrated to the kitchen, where they split into groups. The twins carried on their conversation at the kitchen table, whilst Sven, Rufus and Andrew formed a group and invited Mitch to join them. This left Marnie with Abigail, Svetlana and Juliana. The latter two dominated the conversation with talks of upcoming holidays, tennis matches, and the usual female tittle-tattle of who did what with whom and where. At least, this is how Marnie viewed such conversations. Abigail asked Marnie how she was settling in, as a way of trying to get her to open up.

Just at that moment, Abigail's mobile rang and she announced that she had to pop back home very briefly. Juliana and Svetlana made their excuses to Marnie and wandered off, leaving her alone. Looking around for Mitch, she saw that he was with the husbands and seemed to be having a good time, so she went outside and stood on the large patio which ran the length of the kitchen and living room. The living room patio doors were open slightly and she could hear female voices. Marnie realised that the voices belonged to Juliana and Svetlana, and that they had simply gone back into the living room. Marnie edged closer to the open doors so that she could hear what they were saying.

'What do you think of the new couple then?'

'Well, he's okay. I wouldn't kick him out of bed. Would you?' This was followed by laughter.

'No, I wouldn't. But her, I don't see the attraction for him. She's so plain and dowdy. Do you see what she's wearing? Do you think she made that dress?'

'I don't know, but she must have had it for years. It's so old-fashioned.'

'I bet she even makes her own curtains.' Both women giggled.

'I doubt it. She probably buys ready-mades. Actually, Juliana, it's quite complicated to make your own. I tried it once. Complete disaster. Who makes yours?'

'Oh, the wonderful woman who owns "Going Off The Rails". She's a wizard at curtain-making. I can give you her number if you want.'

'Oh, yes please. I fancy a change. Shall we go and top our drinks up and see what the boys are up to?'

Marnie had heard enough and was mortified. She decided she would head home. This get-together wasn't quite her thing in any event, but she knew she had to endure such things for the sake of her marriage and future financial stability. Catching Mitch's eye, she signalled she was off. He understood, and she knew he had to stay behind because this was essential networking for him. As Marnie was leaving, Abigail was coming back in.

'Leaving already?' she asked.

'Yes, I'm a bit tired,' Marnie replied.

'I suspect these kinds of gatherings aren't quite your thing. Am I right?'

Marnie smiled. 'Spot on. I'd much rather be at home with a cup of tea and watching *Coronation Street* or *Emmerdale*.' She shrugged her shoulders.

'If you're free on Monday afternoon, come to mine for a cup of tea. I have to leave at 3:30 to pick the girls up from school, so how does 2 o'clock sound? It will be just the two of us. Okay?'

'That would be great. Thank you. See you Monday,' replied Marnie, and she went home feeling much happier.

By the time Mitch got back, Marnie was asleep, and he didn't want to wake her. He had learnt a few things about his new neighbours. They were all obviously very wealthy, and very self-satisfied. The only one out of the men who didn't work was Rufus, who told Mitch that he had worked in the City for a number of years, made a ton of money, and retired, "old boy". These days, he spent his time playing golf, going to the gym, and – tapping the side of his nose – every Friday going to London for an old boys' day out, at which Sven and Andrew looked at each other and laughed.

Sven, Mitch had learnt, was a senior partner in a law firm in London which dealt with shipping law which, Mitch thought, explained his serious demeanour. As for Andrew, Mitch found him a touch hard work and self-important. It wasn't that he was unfriendly, and Mitch felt one of his alliterations coming on, it was just that he was disinterested, detached and dismissive. He owned his own software company that had contracts with large government agencies which, Andrew had explained somewhat pompously, he wasn't allowed to name or discuss.

Mitch had asked what the twins did and was answered by Andrew who had simultaneously wrinkled his nose and sniffed and replied, 'Oh, they run a software company as well. Not in the same league as my company, of course, and much smaller, but they appeal to the general market and make a good living from it. No competition for me.' He then laughed.

Then, the conversation turned towards Mitch. Rufus had asked Mitch what he did to "earn his crust". Without missing a beat, Mitch replied, 'Timeshare and, before you ask, no it's not selling one-week shares in Tenerife or Madeira. I'm much more upmarket than that. I own my own yacht timeshare company. I could give you the sales spiel, but this isn't the right time. If any of you are interested, let me know and I'll drop a leaflet round.'

'That's something I'd be interested in,' said Rufus. 'Got a lot of time on my hands now, and I'm sure it would appeal to Juliana. Drop some information in next time you're passing.'

Sven and Andrew had also expressed interest. Sometimes Mitch did feel as if God was on his side. He hadn't expected this to have happened so quickly and had not even gotten round to thinking up the leaflet. However, an opportunity had presented itself and Mitch was not about to let it pass. 'I've got an idea,' he said to the assembled group, 'how do you boys feel about a day out on one of my yachts? This will give you an idea of what you can expect. No girls, though. Just us boys.'

'That sounds like a jolly good idea,' replied Rufus. 'Sven, Andrew, are you up for that?' Sven and Andrew both nodded their assent.

'Do you think Tommy and Toby would be interested?' asked Mitch, looking over at the table where they were sitting with their wives, deep in conversation.

'I'll ring them tomorrow and get back to you,' said Rufus.

'Brilliant. Thanks, Rufus. I was thinking maybe in a couple of weeks' time. Probably a Saturday. Now I'd better say goodbye and get back to the wife.'

*

Mitch was going to tell Marnie about his unexpected success over breakfast, but Marnie got in first and told Mitch what she had overheard Juliana and Svetlana saying about her. 'That was why I left early, because I was feeling so upset.' However, she had surprised Mitch because, rather than sitting glumly at the table feeling sorry for herself, she showed a streak of assertiveness which was quite unlike her. 'Mitch, you once said to me that we were in a "sink or swim" situation, and that you were not about to sink. Well, neither am I. I am not going to let the comments of those mean over-pampered women upset me. I have gone along with everything you have wanted until now, but things have got to change. I would like some money, please, to go shopping, and I'm going by myself so that I choose which shops I go into and what I buy. Are you okay with that?'

Mitch was completely taken aback. He had never seen such a show of spirit coming from Marnie and could only respond with, 'Yes, of course. Anything you say. But, Marnie, please don't go too mad. Where do you think you'll shop?'

'Probably Knighton. There's a good selection of shops, and you needn't worry that I'll break the bank.'

'Let me know how much you need, and I'll withdraw some money. Now I really must get on with my work. I was going to tell you what I found out last night, but you've delayed me with your demands. A cup of coffee in half an hour would be great.' Mitch exited the kitchen and went upstairs to the back bedroom which doubled up as a study.

The time spent at the party had been worthwhile for Mitch. Not only could he now put names to the faces he had seen coming and going from their houses, he was also beginning to get some idea of the neighbourhood dynamics. The ones who had already "made it" were in the group he had spent time with in the kitchen, comprising Rufus, Sven and Andrew. From his surveillance, he realised that Sven and Andrew were neighbours who lived in adjacent large, detached houses built on sizeable plots.

Rufus and Juliana's house, which was on the opposite side of the road and towards the middle end of the road, was one of the largest and could be described as a mansion and had both a swimming pool and tennis court in the grounds. The house next door to them, which was currently empty, was also an older-style mansion and Mitch recognised it as the one he discarded when looking to rent because it was too large for his and Marnie's needs, and too expensive. The only two houses left in that part of the road, and which were built on one plot, with a shared driveway and post box, were owned by the twins and their wives. Both houses were constructed to a very modern design and built predominantly of glass and steel, with some token brickwork. However, even though large by any other standard, they were the smallest in that part of the road. From this, Mitch drew the conclusion that the ones who were still aspiring to climb the social ladder were the twins who had not really socialised with the others that much and had sat together at the kitchen table.

Mitch's daily surveillances since moving in were also beginning to bear fruit of another kind, which is how he knew that Rufus was not where his wife, Juliana, would have thought he was on Wednesday mornings. Depending on whether Rufus was carrying a bag of golf clubs and dressed in plus fours, or wearing a tracksuit and carrying a gym bag, which, Mitch recognised, was the same luxury brand as Fiona's overnight bag, told Mitch that it was either a golfing or gym day. The one exception was a Friday when he would leave the house very smartly dressed and walk to the station. At the party, Mitch had learned from Rufus that this was his day out in London. However, every Wednesday morning – which was supposedly a gym day given that he wore a tracksuit – he would drive away in his dark green Jaguar F-Pace as usual, then obviously park his car somewhere out of sight because Mitch saw Rufus walk back into Green Park Road and go into Sven and Svetlana's house.

Mitch knew that Sven left the house every morning at 7am without exception. Also, from his surveillance, he knew that Svetlana would leave the house at 9:30am on a Tuesday and Friday for her morning run, and on Monday and Thursday mornings she was obviously going to the exercise classes at the village hall, as evidenced by her carrying an exercise mat and a bottle of water. The only morning she stayed at home was on a Wednesday. So, putting two and two together, it was clear to Mitch that Rufus and Svetlana got together on Wednesday mornings for a secret tryst.

Juliana also appeared to be up to something on Fridays but, for now, Mitch gave her the benefit of the doubt as it could be completely innocent. He doubted it, though. He had noticed that after Rufus had left the house at 10am, for his day out in London, Juliana would receive a visit from a young man at 11am. He would be dressed in sportswear and carrying a sports bag, and so Mitch reasonably assumed this could be a personal trainer or tennis coach, as Juliana was the type of woman to have one. This, he decided, would need further investigation.

The twins' wives were constantly coming and going in their matching white Range Rovers and appeared to lead a life of leisure. He assumed they made regular visits to hair and beauty salons, as they were always impeccably groomed. He knew for certain that on a Monday and Thursday morning they went respectively to Zumba and yoga at the village hall because he could see them walking up the road each carrying a mat and water bottle.

The only one of the wives who seemed to lead a busy life that wasn't solely based on leisure was Abigail. Every morning she would drive her two girls, which Mitch had learnt were called Araminta and Arabella, to school, returning at about 10am. On Thursday mornings, she also went to the yoga class. On the mornings of Monday, Wednesday and Friday, she would leave the house at 10:30am, and walk towards the other end of the road. He later discovered that she worked as a volunteer at the care home. Every afternoon, she would pick the girls up from school and bring them home.

Having now got a good idea of his neighbours' routines, he could turn his attention to getting the boys' day out organised and begin work on the leaflet. He heard Marnie coming up the stairs with his coffee. 'Here's your coffee, Mitch. I'm off out.'

'Where are you off to?'

'I thought I'd catch the bus into Cornham and buy some cookery books so that I can cook us something a bit more adventurous for dinner and get to grips with using both ovens. I'll be back in time to get lunch ready.'

Mitch heard the front door closing and turned his attention back to searching the internet. There were quite a few companies with an online presence offering the services he was looking for, with prices determined by the level of luxury required. Having decided that his budget would allow for a mid-priced package, he then decided on the location. Many of the yacht hire companies were based in Chichester, West Sussex, which he immediately disregarded as he was done and dusted with Sussex. The other companies were dotted around the Hampshire area, and he found one near Southampton offering just what he wanted and within his budget. He called the company and the person he spoke to informed Mitch that the cost of hiring a yacht for a day's sailing would cost a "a very reasonable £2,300".

'£2,300!' exclaimed Mitch.

'Well, sir, this is very reasonable. Everything is included to make your day's sailing comfortable and enjoyable. The price includes a skipper, luxury food hamper, wine, beer and soft drinks. If you want other alcoholic beverages, they would, of course, be extra. Likewise, with the food. For an extra charge, we can supply you with your very own chef to cook a delightful gourmet lunch.'

'No, no, it's okay. Beer and wine, and a hamper will do. How much notice do you need?'

'Well, you're in luck,' the man had replied. 'We're not yet in the high season and so I could organise a trip for you with at least a week's notice. And I must tell you, that the price goes up considerably once the season gets underway.'

'Okay. I'll get back to you as soon as possible. Do I need to pay a deposit?'

'No, that's fine, sir. Just get back to me with a date and I'll make sure you and your friends have a brilliant day's sailing.'

Although Mitch had baulked at the amount of money he was going to have to spend, he reminded himself that it was all for a good cause and he was actually looking forward to the day out. He really did feel as if he had come up in the world. Just then, his mobile phone rang. He didn't recognise the number but answered it anyway with a curt, 'Hello.'

'Cliff, old boy, it's Rufus.'

'Ah, Rufus. Hello.'

'As promised, I spoke to the twins about a day's sailing and also sounded them out about your yacht timeshare thing. They're very keen.'

'That's brilliant news. Thank you, Rufus. I was thinking about Saturday 14th, if that suits everyone.'

'I'm sure that will be fine. Leave it with me, old boy, and I'll rally the troops and get back to you.'

'Fantastic! I'll be dropping a leaflet off soon with more information. The current brochure is still at the printers,' Mitch added as an afterthought. 'Well, must get back to it. Got to earn money if I'm to keep the wife happy.'

Rufus laughed. 'You're right there. Happy wife, happy life. That's my motto. Cheerio.'

The morning passed quickly, and it was lunchtime. Mitch heard the front door open and close which signalled Marnie's return from Cornham. He went downstairs and found her in the kitchen, where two carrier bags were on the kitchen table. One bore the name of the supermarket-cum-delicatessen she had previously refused to go into, and the other of the local bookshop.

'What's all this, Marnie? And I see you've been to the supermarket you refused to go into!' said Mitch in surprise.

Marnie smiled. 'Yes, I have, haven't I? So, I went to the bookshop, and I bought two cookery books for beginners. Then, I went and had a coffee, and found an easy recipe in one of the books for tonight's dinner.

I know how busy you are, and that you don't like being interrupted, so I thought I'd brave it and go into that supermarket to see if I could get the ingredients to save you the trouble of having to drive me somewhere. Didn't I do well?'

'You did indeed. And how was it? Was it as bad as you thought?'

Marnie shrugged her shoulders. 'Of course not. It's just an ordinary supermarket, but with some odd food. People have different tastes, I suppose. I also went to the delicatessen section to get us something for lunch, and that's what I need to get on with now.'

'What are we having, because I'm starving?'

Marnie aimed for what she thought was a nonchalant look. 'We're having sweet potato and feta cheese scotch egg, with onion marmalade, and a rocket leaf salad dressed with olive oil and balsamic drizzle.'

'Bloody hell, Marnie, you'll be applying for MasterChef next.' He was tempted to ask what she would be serving up for dinner but decided he would probably be better off not knowing.

Marnie turned away with a grin and went to prepare lunch. Having now made the trip into Cornham by herself on the bus and taken the plunge and gone into two of its independent shops, and one of its cafés, she felt a sense of achievement and a rise in her level of confidence. Mitch, on the other hand, although pleased that Marnie was coming out of her shell and becoming more adventurous in the kitchen – although regrettably not in the bedroom – didn't want her to become too self-assured or independent. The dynamic of their relationship worked perfectly for him, and he didn't want anything rocking the boat.

*

It was Monday morning. Mitch was upstairs whilst Marnie was in the kitchen looking through her cookery books and planning that night's evening meal. After lunch, she announced that she had been invited to Abigail's for a cup of tea and would see him later.

'Okay,' he replied. 'Have a nice time. See if you can find out anything interesting. Oh, and, by the way, you should go to yoga on Thursday mornings. Abigail goes and so do Tammy and Trixie, and Svetlana.'

At the mention of Svetlana, Marnie wrinkled her nose. 'I haven't got anything suitable to wear,' she said as she turned to go.

'You only need a T-shirt and leggings, and you've got plenty of those. But you'd better buy yourself a yoga mat. Anyway, enjoy your *afternoon* tea and girly gossip. Some of us have to go back to work.'

Marnie raised her eyes up to the ceiling and exited the kitchen. 'Bye, Mitch. Love you,' she shouted from the doorway.

'Er, love you too, Marnie,' said Mitch, slightly nonplussed, as terms of endearment and expressions of affection were not usually on Mitch and Marnie's menu.

It was mid-afternoon, and Mitch heard the front door shut. Going down the stairs, he headed into the kitchen to find Marnie. He knew she would be in there because it had become her favourite part of the house. 'So, how did it go?' he asked.

'It went very well. She's nice and down to earth and didn't ask too many questions. Their house is odd, though.'

'What do you mean, "odd"?'

'Well, you know how laid-back Abigail is, I thought their house would be very homely with a "lived-in" look. It was nothing like that. It was like a show house. Exceptionally clean and tidy. In fact, there was nothing out on the surfaces anywhere, not even in the kitchen. It actually looked as if no one lived in it. Also, I thought Abigail would be one of those domestic types. You know, always baking cookies and wearing an apron covered in flour.

'Yes, I would have thought that too. Isn't she?'

'No, doesn't appear to be. And I had to laugh, because I thought I was bad enough in only knowing how to use one oven at a time, but she doesn't even know how to use her oven at all. It's one of those posh ones. What are they called? Begins with the letter "A"… Agas! That's it, she has an Aga and it's a bright turquoise colour. In fact, the colour matches the fridge-freezer, which also has an odd name. Not to my taste at all. Far too bright, but probably very expensive. Now, where was I… Oh yes, she's never cooked with her oven. Evidently, she asked Andrew if she could change it for a traditional one, but he said no.'

'What does she do then?'

'Well, you're going to be very surprised. She uses a microwave, "slow cooker", and the rest is cooked on a mini grill. One of those George Formby things.'

Mitch burst out laughing.

Marnie frowned. 'What are you laughing at?'

'You mean George Foreman, silly. George Formby was a very popular singer and comedian who played the ukulele. Anyway, I bet the house reflects Andrew's taste. He gives the impression of being one of those uptight, prissy people.'

'I also asked her about the residents of Green Park Estate, and if they belonged to the Green Park Road community. It occurred to me, Mitch, that they might prove useful for our project.'

Mitch noticed that Marnie had said "our" and not "your", which she normally did. He let this pass and praised her instead for her initiative. 'What did she say?' he asked.

'She said that the residents of Green Park Estate had their own community and did not mix with any of the residents of Green Park Road. She said that they were all very secretive and kept themselves to themselves. She said that she rarely saw the gates open and imagined it must be like living in a commune. She's offered to take me shopping to Knighton. Also, she does voluntary work at the care home at the end of the road. She suggested I might like to volunteer. Evidently, they need people to come in for a few hours a week to chat to the old folk, play games and read to them. I'd like to do that, Mitch. Sorry, I've gabbled on a bit, haven't I?'

'Yes, Marnie, you have, and you need to calm down. As for doing voluntary work at the care home, I suppose that's all right, but I don't want you getting too attached to the old people like you did with those kids in Luton when you were playing at being mum. I can see you get easily involved, and playing at being a surrogate doting daughter can only lead to disappointment.'

Marnie had gone very quiet and red in the face. 'You can be so mean sometimes. You should think before you speak, Mitch Mitchelson. It's because of you that I never became a mother, and now you're suggesting I want to play at being a "doting daughter", as you put it. May I remind you, which you seem to have forgotten with your insensitive remarks, that I never had a chance to "play", as you put it, at being a "doting daughter" because my mum died before I had a chance, and my dad – who you never met, because if he had met you he would never have given his permission for you to marry me—' Marnie paused mid-flow to draw breath, and Mitch seized his chance.

'Marnie, calm down, calm down…'

174

'Shut up, Mitch. I haven't finished speaking. Now, where was I? Oh yes, my father died when I was very young, and, oh bugger, I've completely lost my train of thought.'

'I think I've got your train of thought, Marnie, very loud and very clear. I'm sorry for my insensitivity. If it makes you happy to do some voluntary work, then go ahead. Can you make me a sandwich? I'm a bit hungry.'

'Okay, I'll see to it. Can I have some money please for when I go shopping?'

'How much do you want?'

Marnie swished her lips from side to side and waggled her head. '£200.'

'Not on your nelly,' said Mitch. 'You can have £100. Bring my sandwich up to me. I'm going back to real work to earn money. Not unpaid "do-gooder" voluntary work.' At the mention of voluntary work, Mitch momentarily wondered how Fiona was getting on.

Marnie and Mitch had an uneasy truce for the rest of the afternoon and kept to separate parts of the house. This suited Mitch because he wanted to focus on designing the leaflet which he would then deliver by hand. It was amazing what could be achieved with templates and fonts in different colours and sizes, which came with his word processing software, and photographs readily available on the internet.

The front of the leaflet contained an image of a large yacht at sea, which Mitch had downloaded from the internet, accompanied by text in large capital letters which Mitch hoped was attention-grabbing – "AHOY THERE!" Beneath that, he typed: "Yacht Ownership Timeshare with PLAIN SAILING", and included an icon of a large wave.

The inside of the leaflet contained what Mitch hoped would be a convincing initial sales pitch:

Ever wanted to own your own yacht, but concerned about the financial commitment and upkeep? YACHT TIMESHARE is the answer. Need to impress clients, or seal a deal? Then look no further – treat them to a day out on YOUR yacht.

Ever had a yearning to sail the Med or cruise the Caribbean with family and friends? YACHT TIMESHARE is the answer.

Ever wanted to watch the sun set with just you and your loved one on board a yacht? Then raise a glass of champagne, because **YACHT TIMESHARE** turns this dream into a reality.

The second page read:

Enjoy owning a yacht at a fraction of the cost

Share the upkeep and the mooring costs, to keep your financial commitment down

MAKE MONEY! You can rent your share out when not using it

On the back page, Mitch wrote: *"IT'S ALL PLAIN SAILING WITH* **PLAIN SAILING** *YACHT OWNERSHIP TIMESHARE.* For more information: contact Cliff Mitchelson".

*

Mitch was pleased with what he had written and had carefully worded the leaflet so as to appeal to his target audience and hopefully cover all bases. He was particularly proud of his use of the title "Yacht Ownership Timeshare", because the capital letter of each word spelt out YOT. Originally, he had come up with the idea of a yacht ownership bond but realised that the first letter of each word spelled YOB which he didn't think would give the right impression for the Green Park Road group. Mitch printed off six leaflets, which was sufficient for his immediate needs.

He went downstairs to find Marnie and found her watching television. 'Is everything good between us, Marnie?' he asked. 'Because I need you fully on board with this project, as it's a biggie.'

'Yes, Mitch, I'm on board. Just don't bully me so much. Don't forget that £100 you promised me,' she replied, rather sulkily.

'I'll get it out for you tomorrow. Is that acceptable, your ladyship?'

'There's no need to be sarky, but yes that's fine. I'd like a bit more for housekeeping as well. This isn't Luton, you know. Everything is that bit more expensive here.'

However, Mitch noticed that she smiled kindly at him, before getting up and walking out of the living room to go into the kitchen to prepare the evening meal.

Mitch didn't sleep very well that night. He had too much on his mind. The yacht timeshare project had happened much quicker than he had expected. Apart from the finished leaflet, which he was pleased with, he hadn't fully thought things through in that he didn't have a real plan for the boys' day out. Then there was the small matter of a change in Marnie's behaviour and attitude towards him. She had begun to assert herself, and answer back and this change, combined with her fledgling independence, unnerved him as he hadn't yet found a way of dealing with it.

He had fallen asleep at one point, only to be woken up by a loud, sharp shriek coming from the garden, which had alarmed him. Quietly getting out of bed, he went to the window and looked out onto the garden below. Two yellow dots peered up at him, making him jump back, until he realised it was a fox. Something else also caught his eye in the road. A car had pulled up outside Andrew and Abigail's house, with the headlights turned off.

Going into the back bedroom, which Mitch had set up as a study, he picked up his binoculars and looked towards the interior of the car. He could just make out two figures leaning in towards each other, and he had a flashback of the first time he had kissed Fiona, which had been in his car outside her apartment block. His attention was brought back to the present by the passenger door opening and the figure of Andrew getting out. He had pressed the entry button on the gate, which subsequently opened, and disappeared inside. The car drove slowly down the road with only the sidelights on.

Interesting, thought Mitch, who found Andrew to be the most impenetrable and aloof one of the group. He also wondered about Abigail and Andrew's relationship. He genuinely liked Abigail, as she behaved kindly and decently towards Marnie. The twins' wives appeared to keep themselves to their own tight unit and, whilst not paying Marnie much attention, at least they weren't unfriendly towards her. The same couldn't be said for Juliana or Svetlana, however, who so far had shown a mean streak in their dismissive attitude towards her.

Making a mental note to keep an eye on Andrew, Mitch returned to bed where he fell instantly asleep.

*

It was the following week, and Mitch's main task was to begin the carefully timed delivery of his leaflets. Marnie was off doing her own thing, having got into a routine. On a Monday and Friday afternoon, she would spend a couple of hours volunteering at the care home. On Monday mornings she went to the Zumba class held in the village hall, and on Thursday mornings, having now purchased a mat, she went to the yoga class. Today, being Wednesday, she had announced that she was off out, and would be back early afternoon and so Mitch would need to get his own lunch. This suited him as he didn't want any time-consuming demands or distractions.

Once Marnie had left, he set off to deliver his leaflets. His first port of call was Sven and Svetlana's house. As per Rufus' schedule on a Wednesday, Mitch had waited until he saw Rufus go into the driveway and let himself in. He knew from his observations that Sven would have left for work at 7am, and that Svetlana would be at home because it was a non-jogging day. Ten minutes later, Mitch rang the doorbell. It opened slightly and he could just make out Svetlana's face.

'Hello. Who is it?'

'It's me, Svetlana – Cliff. I'm dropping off some information that Sven expressed interest in. Is everything okay?'

The door opened wider to reveal Svetlana dressed in a maid's outfit, wearing pink rubber gloves and holding a pink feather duster, which she waggled at Mitch with a cheeky grin.

'Crikey, Svetlana, is that how you dress to do your housework? Sven is a lucky boy, or is it someone else you're going to give a dusting to?'

'You have a naughty twinkle in your eye, Cliff. What is this information for Sven?'

'Yacht timeshare. He said to drop my leaflet round. I'm off to give one to Rufus now, or perhaps you could give it to him?'

Svetlana looked at the person she knew as Cliff for a moment, clearly not sure how to respond. Finally, she said, 'Okay, I'll give him a leaflet as well. This is our secret. Don't you dare tell anyone.' And she put a finger on her pouting, glossy, pink lips.

'I won't, Svetlana. Mum's the word. Just give Sven and Rufus the leaflet for me and persuade them what a good idea it is. If Rufus asks any questions, just say that I saw him coming into your driveway and assumed he was visiting Sven.'

Svetlana closed the door, and Mitch walked down the driveway whistling. He dropped a leaflet off in Andrew and Abigail's post box and put two leaflets in the twins' shared post box. Although he had given Svetlana a leaflet for Rufus, he had every intention of going to see if Juliana was in. She was.

'Oh, hello, Cliff. If it's Rufus you're after, he's at the gym.'

'Likes his exercise, doesn't he? I often see him with his golf or gym bag. Must be nice to be retired. Look, can you give him this leaflet. He wanted some more information about my business.'

Juliana took the leaflet and looked closely at it. 'What's this about? Oh, how interesting. I've always wanted to go sailing around the Mediterranean. Rufus is always going on about taking a cruise, but I'm not keen. It would just be like a floating hotel, and one never knows what the other passengers would be like, if you get my drift.'

'I do, Juliana. With yacht timeshare, you get to choose who you sail with. Well, I must be off.'

Mitch knew that Rufus would be initially confused when Svetlana gave him the leaflet, and then he would be perturbed because he would have realised that Cliff (as Rufus knew him to be called) knew that he had been with Svetlana whilst Sven was at work. He would have then gone home, and Juliana would have given Rufus the second leaflet, which probably confused him again until the penny dropped. At some instinctive level, he would have realised that he had been rumbled because he could hardly have said to Juliana that he already had a leaflet. Also, with Juliana showing a keen interest in his yacht timeshare, Mitch knew he was onto a winner.

Having achieved what he set out to do, he walked back to the house and began work on drawing up a feasible financial scheme for his sales pitch. He looked on a number of websites, did the maths, and drew up what he considered to be a worthwhile plan, which would earn sufficient income for him and Marnie to live on wherever they next chose to live, whilst making it more than affordable for the group to seriously consider buying into. He had been so engrossed in what he was doing that he had forgotten all about lunch and when he heard the front door shut, which told him that Marnie was back from wherever she had been, he realised it must be early afternoon.

'I'm upstairs, Marnie,' he shouted.

'Come down, Mitch. I've got something to show you,' she shouted back.

Mitch went downstairs to the kitchen. Marnie was standing in the centre of the room, looking very pleased with herself. Doing a twirl, and patting her hair, she said, 'Well, what do you think?'

It took Mitch a moment to see the difference. Marnie had been growing her usually short brown hair a bit longer over the past few weeks, and he now noticed that it was styled very nicely and not dissimilar, in shape, to the hairstyle worn by his cousin Vicky, and Fiona. His attention was then drawn to the blonde streaks that had been added which had lightened up her natural colour and created a look that was both fashionable and attractive.

'Well,' she repeated, 'what do you think?'

'Very nice, Marnie. Very nice indeed.'

'Also, look at this.' Marnie lifted up her top and showed Mitch how loose the waistband of her trousers was. 'I've lost weight!' She sidled up to Mitch and turned to face him. 'Some of my clothes are a bit on the big side now, so can I have the money you promised me, and I can tell Abigail so that she can take me into Knighton.'

Because everything was going according to plan, Mitch was feeling very upbeat and generous. 'Okay, Marnie, but I can take you shopping tomorrow if you like?'

Stepping back, Marnie lifted up her chin slightly, 'Well, it will have to be in the afternoon because I go to yoga in the morning.'

Normally, Mitch would have answered with a "it's tomorrow morning or never" response, but he was liking the "new-look" Marnie and so he agreed. Marnie, who expected a response such as "it's tomorrow morning or never", was taken aback but nevertheless pleased.

The following morning, Marnie saw Abigail at the yoga class and thanked her for offering to take her shopping, but "Cliff" had said he would go with her. 'And that way,' she had added, 'I can get more money out of him. Do you mind?'

'No, not at all, Marnie,' Abigail had replied. 'And get as much as you can out of him,' she had said with a laugh.

Thursday afternoon had proved to be a pleasant shopping trip to Knighton, and Marnie was pleased with her purchases. Having kept within the budget set by

Mitch, as a further treat, he said he would take her to the local pub for a meal. She went upstairs to get changed into one of her new outfits and came down the stairs wearing the jersey wrap dress she had chosen, which, because she had lost weight, showed off her newly toned figure. The colours of the dress were mint green, pale pink and cream. The outfit was completed with cream shoes and matching handbag, which Marnie had seen on sale in a shoe shop that was closing down. When Mitch saw what Marnie was wearing, he experienced a jolt because with her newly blonde-highlighted hair, which was now styled in a fashionable bob, he had another brief flashback of Fiona.

'You look nice, Marnie. Hold on, I've got a present for you, which will finish your new outfit off perfectly.' He ran up the stairs and retrieved from the study the earrings he had given to Fiona, but which he had taken back when he had left Hove.

'Close your eyes, and open your hands,' he instructed her. Then he placed the box in her hands and told her to open her eyes.

'Ooh, what's this?' she asked, completely taken aback because Mitch rarely, if ever, bought her presents outside of Christmas or birthdays. She opened the box and saw the silver and green tasselled earrings.

'What do you think?' asked Mitch. 'Do you like them?'

'They're very nice, Mitch. Just one problem, though.'

Mitch jutted out his chin. 'What's that, then?'

'They're for pierced ears. I don't have pierced ears,' replied Marnie, looking at Mitch suspiciously.

Fuck, he thought. 'Oh, silly me,' he said, hitting his forehead with the palm of his hand. 'Sorry, Marnie. I just assumed you had pierced ears. Most women seem to have them these days.'

Marnie narrowed her eyes at him. 'Well, firstly, I'm not "most women" and secondly, have you ever seen me wearing earrings, Mitch?'

'Er, no, I haven't,' he replied nervously.

'That's because I don't have pierced ears, and clip-ons pinch.'

'Well, you know me, I'm not that observant, so…'

'What do you mean, you're "not that observant"? You clearly are observant because you said that – and I quote – "most women seem to have them these days".'

Sensing he was losing the battle and getting himself into deep water, he put on a defeated look and held his arms out. 'Look, we'll find somewhere that does ear piercing and get them done. How does that sound?'

Somewhat placated, Marnie replied, 'That sounds like a good idea, and then I'll be able to wear these lovely earrings you bought.'

Marnie wasn't stupid and knew he had bought them for someone else but, for whatever reason, had hung onto them. They were very fashionable and so she wasn't about to give them back and put them in her handbag.

'Oh, by the way,' she said as they were leaving the house.

'Yes, Marnie?'

'Have you forgotten that you owe me a replacement engagement ring? A big one. We can shop for that on the same day I get my ears pierced. Now, let's go and eat. I'm really hungry.'

Bloody women, thought Mitch. *Never satisfied. You get them one thing, and then they want something else.* As he drove away, he wondered what Fiona had done with the engagement ring he had given her. Marnie, sitting quietly in the passenger seat, was also wondering what had happened to her engagement ring. She also had an inkling that the earrings had probably been purchased for the same woman. She knew, however, never to ask too many questions about what Mitch got up to.

It was Friday morning, and Marnie was getting ready to go to the care home having changed her shift from the afternoon.

'If you can hang on a minute, Marnie, I'll walk down with you as I'm off to see Rufus,' said Mitch, knowing full well that Rufus would be out because it was his London day, but that Juliana would be in.

Although they didn't hold hands walking down the road, they walked side by side, which was not the norm for them, as usually Mitch walked at least four steps ahead of Marnie, leaving her trailing behind. As they approached Rufus and Juliana's driveway, a young man was seen entering the house.

'I wonder who that is,' said Marnie. 'He looks very fit. Perhaps he's her personal trainer.' Marnie grinned at Mitch and raised her eyebrows expectantly.

'The answer is no, Marnie. You cannot have a personal trainer. Just do more Zumba or yoga. Now off you go to the old folks' home. See you later.' And he gave her a peck on the cheek and a pat on the behind.

Mitch walked up to the front door and rang the bell. Juliana opened the door. She was wearing a black and orange striped onesie, complete with hood and two pointed ears. *Hell's bells,* thought Mitch, *has the woman got no shame dressing like that at her age.* Instead, he said, 'Is Rufus in, Juliana?'

'Um, no, he isn't. Was that Marnie I just saw?' she said somewhat distractedly.

'Yes. She helps out at the care home,' he replied.

Juliana nodded and stuck her bottom lip out. 'Oh, is she a carer then? Well, that doesn't surprise me.'

Mitch didn't like the tone of Juliana's voice and, frowning slightly, asked, 'What do you mean, Juliana?' Before she could answer, Mitch continued because he wanted to avoid getting into an argument with her as he needed her co-operation for his project. 'Actually, Juliana, Marnie does voluntary work there. It was Abigail who suggested it because she also volunteers at the home.'

Juliana sniffed. 'Oh, well, I see.'

'By the way,' said Mitch, 'did I see a young man go into your house just now? Is that your son?'

Juliana looked at him. 'We only have a daughter. That's… Marcus. He's my personal trainer. Now, I must go as I'm in the middle of my fitness session.'

Before Juliana shut the door, a male voice from inside said, 'Pussy cat, where are you? Here, pussy, pussy. Come and get your treat.'

Juliana closed the door, but not before Mitch heard her say "miaow", or maybe it was "ciao". Nevertheless, it had pleased Mitch to see that she had looked discomfited.

He began to make his way back home. Passing the twins' houses, the gates opened and one of the Range Rovers came out, driven by one of the wives. They waggled their fingers at him in a wave and grinned, revealing bright white teeth. As he passed Sven and Svetlana's house, he heard, 'Cliff, cooee, Cliff.' Looking up, he saw Svetlana calling to him from an open upstairs window. 'Hold on,' she shouted, 'I'm coming down.'

The gates opened and Svetlana stood in the open doorway. She was wearing a bright pink and sky-blue kimono, which was tied loosely at the waist, and pink velvet slippers. 'I've got good news for you, Cliff. I've persuaded Sven and Rufus to seriously consider investing in your yacht timeshare scheme. You have no idea what I had to do to get Rufus to agree.'

'Don't you mean Sven, your husband, Svetlana?'

186

'No. He's not bothered. He's strictly a "meat and two veg" kind of man, once a month. Anything I want, I get, because he knows how lucky he is to have me. Rufus, on the other hand, although he is old, is far more demanding and adventurous.'

'Don't you worry about him having a heart attack, Svetlana?'

'Don't be silly, Cliff. I'm very good at using my mouth for resuscitation purposes.' And she winked when she said this.

At the thought of Svetlana's plump lips in the act of resuscitating *him*, Mitch momentarily experienced a slight loss of composure when an image popped into his mind, but he recovered sufficiently to ask, 'And what about Juliana? Has she any idea of what you and Rufus get up to?

'Listen, Juliana knows all about Rufus's peccadilloes. She just doesn't know that I'm one of them. Anyway, she's no angel. As the saying goes, "while the cat's away, the mouse will play". Now, where's my reward?'

Actually, thought Mitch, *it's the other way around. Whilst the mouse is away, the cat will play.* 'You'll get your reward once they've both signed on the dotted line.'

Svetlana pouted. 'They've all but signed, Cliff. I'd like my reward now. I'm not known for my patience.' She opened the door fully to allow him to enter, giving him her best "come hither" smile.

'I can't, Svetlana. Marnie is expecting me back.'

'No she isn't. I saw Abigail earlier. She told me she was going to the care home and that your wife would be there as well.'

'Well, I promised I would see Rufus about something.'

'You are a silly boy, Cliff. You have just come from that direction, and Rufus would have told you that Friday is the day he goes up to London. This frees Juliana up, and Friday is Juliana's "dressing up" day, if you know what I mean?'

'I don't think I do, Svetlana.'

'Well, come in and I'll explain it to you.' And she pulled him inside.

They were in the bedroom, and Svetlana had made Mitch take off his clothes and lie on the bed. 'Here, Cliff, put this blindfold on.'

'Hold on,' he said, 'I'm not into kinky stuff, Svetlana, and I'm certainly not putting on a blindfold or handcuffs.'

'Don't be boring, Cliff. Just pop the blindfold on, lie there and be quiet.' Mitch could hear a drawer opening and closing, and a rustling sound. 'Okay, take off the blindfold.'

Mitch sat up and removed the blindfold, surprised to see Svetlana wearing a red and white Sexy Santa outfit, which was a bit incongruous as it was May. 'Ta-dah,' she said, flinging her arms wide open, which caused the front of her cape to open and fall to the floor. Svetlana was wearing (if, indeed, it could be called wearing) two fluffy white pompoms attached to her nipples, and red furry knickers trimmed with white. Climbing onto the bed she opened her legs wide. Mentally processing that she was wearing crotchless knickers, physically he sprang into action and climbed on top of her.

His almost-last words to her were, 'Svetlana, make sure you don't scratch me with those talons of… Ouch!'

'Shush, Cliff. Do you like this?'

'Oh, yes, very nice. Just lift your hips up a bit higher.'

Sex with Svetlana proved to be an energetic and not unenjoyable experience, which brought back memories of Fiona. Like Fiona, she knew all the right moves. Unlike Fiona, she was noisy and demanding. Mitch was exhausted and looked forward to a quiet and lazy afternoon with Marnie. He also needed to take a shower and hoped that Marnie was still at the care home.

His hopes were dashed when he saw that there was a van in the driveway which he didn't recognise. On entering into the hallway, he was greeted with female laughter coming from the kitchen, then a male voice, and then more laughter. As Marnie rarely laughed, it took Mitch a few moments before he realised it was Marnie laughing.

An attractive, muscular young man was in the kitchen, talking about mowing the lawn and trimming the bushes. Mitch could have sworn the young man had winked at Marnie when he said this. Marnie was laughing and simpering, which was totally out of character.

'Hello, and who is this then?' asked Mitch.

'This is Dominic, the gardener.'

Dominic extended his hand. 'You must be Cliff. Did the agent not tell you that the owners pay me to come in and tend to the garden every couple of months?'

'No, he didn't. So this has come as a surprise. What is it you do exactly, apart from mowing the lawn and trimming the bushes?'

'Well, I also do any weeding, give the garden a good watering, and generally look after the plants. I don't need to bother you, as I let myself in through the side gate as I have a key.'

'Okay, well as long as I don't have to pay, that's fine. When do you think you will be coming?'

'Is Monday convenient?'

'Yes, no problem. Let me show you out.' As Mitch turned to walk Dominic out, he saw that Dominic had winked again at Marnie who had instantly blushed and giggled.

At the front door, Mitch said he would see Dominic on Monday morning as arranged, adding, 'My wife will not be here, so there won't be anything to distract you from your work.'

Mitch went back into the kitchen. 'He's coming Monday morning, whilst you're at the Zumba class. I shall be here in any case. I didn't like the way you were flirting with him. It's quite out of character for you. By the way, what were you laughing at when I came in?'

'Oh, he was talking about why he liked gardening, and he said the best bit was planting seeds and then watching them grow. He said it was just like making a baby, and then realised what he'd said and put his hand over his mouth. It made me laugh, because he was clearly embarrassed.'

'I can't leave you alone for five minutes, can I? Here I am, just back from a very stressful and tiring morning, to find you flirting with *Dominic, the gardener,* and talking about making babies. You really are a bit gullible at times. He knew exactly what he was saying. I'm surprised he didn't come right out with it and ask if he could plant his seed in you!'

'Don't be so disgusting!' shouted Marnie, who had gone red in the face.

Mitch could see quite clearly where this talk about making babies might lead to and so cut her off before she could continue. 'It's not good enough, Marnie. Where's my lunch? Bring it up to me in my study. Some of us have *more* work to do!' Mitch left the kitchen and stomped up the stairs, muttering under his breath about new hairstyles and gigolo gardeners.

Well, I never, thought Marnie, *he's jealous.* She smiled to herself, and then she felt sad because she hadn't grown any babies and never would. However, Dominic had flirted with her which made her happy, and she had flirted back, enjoying the attention, because usually men took no notice of her whatsoever, including her husband.

*

It was the week of the boat trip and Mitch was fine-tuning his sales pitch. He had gone over the costings numerous times, which were based on information gleaned from various timeshare websites. He believed he had come up with a package that was more than financially viable for his "clients", whilst earning sufficient money for him and Marnie to live on for the foreseeable future.

The week went by quickly, and Mitch told Marnie that he would be leaving early on Saturday so as to get to where the yacht was moored before the others arrived. He instructed her not to say anything to the other wives, should they approach her for information. Very decently, Rufus had offered him a lift on Saturday, along with Sven, but he had explained that he would make his own way there so as to make sure everything was in "tip-top" form. Tommy and Toby were travelling down together, which left Andrew. Mitch assumed Andrew would travel with Rufus and Sven but was informed that he too was travelling separately.

Saturday arrived and Mitch set off for the outskirts of Southampton. He arrived at the marina where the yacht he had hired was moored, and introduced himself to the skipper who was called Max. The yacht was impressive. Having never been on one before, he was blown away at how luxurious and spacious it was below and above deck. For some reason, he had imagined it would be a bit cramped. In fact, and this is what he couldn't quite grasp, the yacht was bigger than the flat him and Marnie had rented in Luton. After looking around and marvelling at the cabins, he disembarked and headed back to the car park to await his guests.

The twins arrived first, followed by Rufus and Sven. The last to arrive was Andrew. They walked in a group to the yacht. Mitch could tell they were as impressed as he was. Sven had been on cruises but acknowledged that having a timeshare would be a different experience altogether. As they were about to board, Andrew's mobile phone rang and a conversation ensued of "yes", "no" and "see you shortly". Eventually hanging up, he turned to the group. 'Sorry, chaps. Something's happened at home, and I'm needed back.' He turned and walked briskly back to his car without even saying goodbye to any of them or apologising to Mitch. Furthermore, Mitch noticed the almost imperceptible nod that occurred between Rufus and Sven, whilst the sound of a departing Andrew whistling reached his ears.

The group was introduced to Max, who told them that once they were on board, they were to sit back, relax, and enjoy their enjoy their day. He outlined the route they would be taking, and then he went on board to prepare for the day's sailing. Mitch hadn't paid extra for a crew member to serve them, as he felt he had already spent enough money, but told the group that he wanted to give them his personal service and that he was at their "beck and call".

He left them relaxing on the deck, whilst he went down to the gleaming galley kitchen, which was part of the large saloon. He was amazed to find that the kitchen was equipped with all kinds of gadgets. There was a fancy coffee machine that came with an assortment of different kinds of coffee in different coloured capsules, which took Mitch a while to figure out how to use. At home, they drank instant coffee, although he had acquired a taste for ground coffee when he had lived with Fiona who had used a cafetière. A large hamper was on the table containing their lunch, and the fridge was stocked with wine, beer and two bottles of champagne, which were a pleasant surprise, as he hadn't ordered them. He saw that a basket of croissants and Danish pastries had also been provided and put the basket on the tray with the coffee and carried it upstairs.

They all appeared to be in a chilled-out mood and, as they drank their coffee, he made quick observations of each one of them. The twins had come dressed in matching nautical clothing – blue and white striped Breton T-Shirts, navy shorts, red, white and blue boat shoes, and white crew hats embroidered with the word "Skipper" on the front. They were engrossed in looking at something on their iPads. Rufus had dressed in his usual uniform of red trousers, blue and white striped shirt, and navy boat shoes with white stitching. He was sprawled out on one of the white leather banquettes, with his white and black captain's hat pulled down over his eyes. The hat was complete with gold braid and had an anchor emblem sewed on in the centre. Sven was reading the *Law Society Review* and had made a nod to being at leisure in that, although he still wore a suit, it was a cream-coloured linen suit, underneath which was a white shirt unbuttoned at the neck. On his feet, he wore brown leather loafers, instead of his usual shiny black leather lace-up shoes.

It was a perfect day. The sun shone, and the sea was calm, and Mitch could see they were enjoying the experience of sailing on the Solent. He was also hoping that they were imagining what it would be like to do this for longer than a day. Nevertheless, he needed to move things on before they became too comfortable and didn't want to be bothered listening to a sales pitch. 'Anyone for champagne before lunch?' he asked. They all said yes, and Mitch went down to the galley and took one of the bottles from the fridge. He found the cupboard where the glasses were kept and took down four champagne flutes which he filled with the champagne. Taking them upstairs, he handed them around. Mitch was drinking water, as he needed to keep a clear head.

'So, just to let you all know, Max will shortly be anchoring the yacht off Newtown Creek in the Isle of Wight, where we will have lunch. Enjoy the bubbly and I'll go and prepare the food. You could, of course, have your own crew to do this for you,' he said with a grin.

The selection in the hamper was plentiful and, as promised, came from a luxury range of locally sourced produce. He placed all the food on a large silver tray and carried it carefully upstairs to the deck. He passed round plates and cutlery and told them to help themselves. Asking if they wanted wine or beer, they all chose beer, which pleased Mitch because he fancied taking the wine home with him, and the remaining bottle of champagne. He decided he would begin his sales pitch whilst they were eating and drinking, because after lunch they would probably be too soporific to pay attention. Rufus, in particular, being the age he was, would no doubt doze off.

Once they had filled their plates, he began his pitch. He hadn't got very far when one of the twins revealed what they had been engrossed with on their iPads.

'We've been searching for your website, or your company, Plain Sailing, and can't find anything.'

'Ah, so that's what you've been doing, and here's me thinking you were playing *Candy Crush* or *Angry Birds*,' said Mitch with a laugh. 'You won't find anything, and there's a reason. I don't advertise on the internet.'

'Why's that, old boy?' said Rufus, suddenly paying attention.

'What I offer,' explained Mitch, 'is a luxury product to discerning clients who can afford to have the best. I am very selective with whom I do business with, as I am not interested in attracting a mass-market clientele.'

'That's gratifying to know,' said one of the twins. 'But we've found quite a few yacht timeshare companies on the internet.'

Mitch thought that, despite their silly matching outfits, these boys weren't stupid. 'Well, lads, you have been doing your due diligence and rightly so. It's true, there are companies advertising on the internet, and I work with some of them. The industry generally wants to maintain and attract a high-end level of customer. What we don't want is the yachting fraternity to end up like some aspects of, say, horseracing. You only have to witness the drunken behaviour of racegoers at what used to be prestigious racecourses to see what would happen if we opened up yachting to all and sundry. This is where I come in. I match suitable, high-net-worth individuals, such as yourselves, and who have the right sort of credentials, with premier yachting companies, such as the one whose yacht you're on now. Does that explain things for you, and perhaps offer some reassurance?'

Rufus, who had been drunk and mildly disorderly more than once at a couple of racecourses, grunted, 'Quite right, too. Got to keep the riff-raff out. Brings the whole tone of the place down.'

Toby, or it might have been Tommy, ploughed on regardless. 'That does explain things, Cliff. Thank you. One more question, just so we've dotted our "I's" and crossed our "t's" before we get down to the financial nitty-gritty. What do you get out of this? Are you commission-based?'

'For heaven's sake, boys,' said Sven, who had obviously been listening but so far had remained silent, 'we're supposed to be on a leisurely and relaxing day out. Nonetheless, Cliff, they're asking pertinent questions. I thought you owned this yacht. Is that not the case?'

Mitch had anticipated questions of this sort and had prepared well. 'In answer to your questions, which are certainly fair and reasonable to ask, I don't work on a commission basis as I'm not an employee. However, although I don't own this yacht outright, I do have a share in it and one other. So, it may be the case that you get to take this yacht out, or the other one. Don't forget, though, with your timeshare, you would get a choice of yachts from the companies who belong to the scheme.'

Sven seemed satisfied with Mitch's response, but the twins were not so easily placated. 'It's Toby speaking, by the way. When it comes to money, and a big chunk of it, probably, we like to know exactly what we're getting involved in. There's nothing wrong with that, is there?'

Mitch sensed a change in the atmosphere. A cold front was creeping in, and the sky had suddenly become overcast, causing ripples in the water and a slight rocking of the yacht. He needed to steer the situation back to calmer waters. 'It's okay. No problem, and I hope I've answered your questions fully and allayed any doubts. In fact, now that money has been mentioned, let me get to the "nitty-gritty". Are you all sitting comfortably?' he asked affably and began his carefully rehearsed sales pitch.

'You will be surprised at how affordable this is, particularly when I break down the figures for you. Per month, and this includes VAT, it comes to as little as £867. This amounts to £10,404 a year. I think you will agree this is very good value, especially when you consider the kind of yacht you will have a timeshare in.

Take this one, for example, 40-foot, three spacious berths which sleep six comfortably, a fully equipped modern kitchen with all the mod cons you need, an upper deck, which you haven't been up to yet – but feel free to do so – and the very large lower deck on which you have been relaxing. All of this for £10,404 a year. However, as I said, myself and the companies I work with like to keep the industry exclusive and the clientele some of the best. So, we ask that prospective clients commit to a three-year membership which would mean a one-off payment of £31,212, which would probably be out of reach for the ordinary person.' Mitch stopped to draw breath and take a sip of water, noting that he had got their attention.

'What do we get for that, then?' asked Sven.

'You get two weeks per year—' Before Mitch could expand, Rufus interrupted him.

'That doesn't seem very much, if I may say so. £10,404 for a two-week holiday seems quite pricey to me.'

'I agree, Rufus,' replied Mitch. 'But this isn't your normal holiday, is it? Imagine you and Juliana are on your own yacht – master and mistress – and here, Mitch winked at Rufus, who reddened slightly – of the high seas. Can you imagine docking at Cannes or Monaco? All eyes on you, wondering who you both are. Treated like celebrities. Juliana would love that, I think. Also, even when you stay at a luxury hotel, you are still surrounded by other people. Unless, of course, you go really exclusive and have a room with your own private pool and a butler, which I can assure you would cost a lot more than £10,404. The level of privacy and exclusivity you would get with your timeshare, which I think is very reasonably priced, is out of most people's pockets. And Sven, can you imagine yourself and Svetlana sailing into Puerto Banus for lunch? You could spend a few hours relaxing, whilst Svetlana goes shopping in Marbella or gets her nails and hair done.'

Mitch could see that Rufus and Sven were clearly thinking about the picture he had painted for them. 'Happy wife, happy life,' he reminded them. 'And you, Toby and Tommy. Sail the Italian Riviera or Greek islands. Dock somewhere chic and expensive, send the girls off shopping, whilst you both kick back and drink some chilled wine or beer, or go swimming, or do a spot of fishing. The choice is yours.' Mitch's throat was getting dry from all the talking, and he took another sip of water.

One of the twins piped up. 'I still think that two weeks a year doesn't seem that long, as Rufus has rightly pointed out.'

Ever diligent, Mitch had anticipated questions of this kind. 'Now, this is where you all have to box clever to make your investment work for you. Tommy and Toby, you combine your weeks so that you get a month's use per year. A whole month! Can you imagine that? Rufus, Sven, I imagine that the four of you sometimes holiday together. Am I right?' Both men nodded in agreement. 'So, the two of you could combine your weeks.'

'In practice, that sounds great,' said Sven. 'But I couldn't possibly take a whole month off.'

'Neither could we,' said the twins in unison. 'We have a company to run.'

'No problem. If, say, you don't use your weeks one year, you can carry them over. Or, alternatively, you could rent out your share. A skippered yacht rents out between £2,000 and £3,000 a week in the low season. In the high season, you can rent out your share for even more money. Look, there's no pressure. Enjoy the rest of the day, then go home and think about it.'

Mitch thought that he had done as much as he could. Drawing on a fishing metaphor, he felt that he had cast his hook, line and sinker, and begun the slow and patient process of reeling them in. Rufus stood up and announced he was off to the upper deck to get a more panoramic view, which signalled to Mitch that he was probably imagining being captain of his own yacht and thinking over the proposal. Sven went back to reading the *Law Society Review*, but Mitch knew he would be mulling over the cost-effectiveness of his investment versus the overall use he would get out of it. Nevertheless, he had made a further nod at being relaxed because he had taken off his loafers and was wiggling his toes. The twins announced they were off to say hello to the skipper, bringing to Mitch's mind the image of small boys who want to go and see the pilot in the cockpit.

The one area where he had been on shaky ground was to do with any questions that may have arisen as to weekend and daily usage. Short of time, he had not been able to fully get to grips with the pro rata costings for this type of use. Thus, he had been dreading any query of this nature. Luckily, the twins had asked their questions, which had taken the conversation off in another direction. Mitch heaved a sigh of relief. All the initial signs were positive, and he felt he could now finally relax. Helping himself to a beer, and a plate of food, he sat back and enjoyed the sun on his face.

On the upper deck, Rufus was indeed imagining he was the captain of his own yacht. He wasn't stupid. He was aware that Cliff knew about him and Svetlana. Whether or not Sven knew was another matter, but he probably wouldn't be that bothered as their marriage was one of convenience, albeit a successful one, which suited them both. With Sven probably only taking one week of his share, Rufus imagined having Juliana on one arm and Svetlana on the other for the remaining weeks. Perhaps, then, a ménage à trois could take place, just as

Svetlana had promised. Not only would he be master of the yacht, but also master in the king-size bed in the master suite.

The yacht returned to its mooring, and everyone disembarked. They all said their goodbyes and promised to get back to him by the end of the week. No one seemed particularly bothered about the cost, and they had all agreed that the financial reward for renting out any unused share was worth consideration. Any uncertainty seemed to arise from the use they would get out of it in the long run.

As Mitch was about to get into his car, Rufus approached him. 'Look here, Cliff, old boy. There's a saying which goes "what goes on board, stays on board", if you know what I mean?'

'I do, Rufus, but in what context?'

'No need to say anything to Marnie about Andrew going AWOL, just in case she says anything to Abigail. If you get my drift?'

'Mum's the word, Rufus. Don't worry, I won't say a dicky bird about anything. Can I leave it to you, then, to explain things to Andrew? You have all the necessary information.'

Rufus winked. 'Leave it with me. I'm sure he'll come on board.'

*

It was only Tuesday morning, but Mitch was on tenterhooks and pacing up and down. One minute he felt buoyant and confident that his project would be a success; the next minute he was feeling anxious and full of doubts. Marnie came down the stairs dressed in a T-shirt, leggings and trainers. 'I thought you'd stopped wearing those sloppy clothes,' said Mitch.

'I have,' Marnie answered brightly. 'I'm off for a jog with Abigail. See you later.' She went over and gave him a quick kiss on the lips and left.

Although Mitch was pleased that Marnie had found a friend in Abigail, he didn't want her getting too attached to either her new friend or lifestyle, because he knew they would be leaving soon, whatever the outcome of his latest project. For now, however, he was happy to let things be. However, his nervous energy prevented him from settling down to do any work. He tried watching morning television but found it all very tedious and some of the presenters incredibly irritating. As it was a nice morning, he thought a walk in the woods might help clear his mind, but whether the walk would calm him down was debateable, because he actually didn't like woods or forests. They were too dark and made him feel claustrophobic and brought back a particular bad memory.

One of the school trips he had gone on was a class visit to the countryside to experience nature, which included a woodland walk. Mitch had needed to find a bush to go behind and got separated from the group. When he had finished, he found that the class had moved on. There was no noise, apart from birdsong and rustling leaves, and he was surrounded by trees. Becoming disorientated, he started shouting for help and then he began to cry. He was found by a teacher who, instead of offering sympathy, told him off for not staying with the group. Worse was to come. His classmates taunted him and began chanting "Cry baby Mitchelson, crying like a girlie". Ever since then, Mitch had steered clear of wooded areas, until today, that was. That schoolboy memory had come back to him so sharp and sudden, that he decided to turn back. Then he heard voices to his left. There was a small clearing with a bench, on which two people were sat. He didn't recognise the woman, but he knew who the man was. It was Andrew. 'Look, I can't just up and leave. You know that. What about the girls?'

'Well, I'm not going to hang about much longer, Andrew. I made it clear from the start that this is serious for me, and not just some fling,' replied the woman, who Mitch detected had an American accent.

Mitch heard Andrew sigh loudly. 'She's a decent woman. Good with the girls, and very attentive to me. Also, think about the money. I would have to give her half of everything, and perhaps even half the house.'

'You should have thought about that. If she's so great, what are you doing with me?'

'What we have is different. It's special. Me and Abi have simply grown apart, and the excitement – if there ever was any – has gone. With you, I feel alive and obviously excited.'

The woman laughed and lent in towards Andrew. Mitch had heard enough and couldn't wait to tell Marnie. He headed back to the house, and then, for some inexplicable reason, decided on the spur of the moment to see if Abigail was back from her jog. As he was nearing her house, he saw Marnie and Abigail jogging down the road together.

Mitch walked up to meet them. 'Ah, Marnie. I saw you from a distance and thought I'd walk up to meet you both.'

'Oh, that's nice of you, Mitch,' said Marnie, and then realised her blunder. Mitch glared at her, and turned towards Abigail and asked how she was, by way of a deflection from Marnie's faux pas.

'Hello, Abigail. How are you?'

'Erm, I'm very well. I'm a bit puzzled, though. Marnie just called you Mitch, or did I hear wrong?'

Mitch had to think on his feet, and fast. 'No, you heard right. Mitchel was my dad's name and, as I resemble him, everyone who knows me from the old days calls me Mitch. To anyone else, my real name is Clifford, shortened to Cliff.'

'Oh, that explains it, then.'

'Did Andrew enjoy the day out on the yacht?' asked Mitch, desperate to change the subject, and knowing full well that Andrew had not gone home that day.

'Oh, yes he did. I've never seen him in such high spirits when he came back,' Abigail replied.

Yes, and I know why, thought Mitch. 'Oh well, I'm glad he enjoyed himself. I suppose he's at work today as usual?'

'No, not today. He's taken the day off and has gone out for a *proper* run in the woods rather than a *jog* around the block. His words, not mine,' she added, rolling her eyes. 'He should be back shortly. Do you want to see him then?'

'No, no, that's okay. No need to mention it either. Just making chit-chat. Well, nice seeing you, Abigail. Come on, Marnie, time for lunch.'

Marnie waved goodbye to Abigail, and said she'd see her later at Juliana's.

'Why are you going to Juliana's later?' asked Mitch.

'I'll tell you when we get back to the house. You're acting a bit weird. What's up? Oh, and I'm sorry about calling you Mitch in front of Abigail.'

'Yep, it's mistakes like that, Marnie, that could cost us dearly. You need to be more careful. Anyway, I got us out of that easily enough. So, I decided to go for a walk in the woods…'

'You don't like woods, Mitch. Why would you do that?'

'I needed to clear my head. Look, there's something I need to tell you. Let's get home, and I'll explain, and then you can tell me why you're going to Juliana's.' Mitch was beginning to develop a stress headache; there was too much going on, and he felt as if everything was unravelling. At that particular moment in time, he wished he had stayed in his comfort zone of romance scams instead of trying to up his stakes and move into the big league. He felt as if he was getting out of his depth but couldn't give up now. The matter was immediately made worse with the appearance of Svetlana, who was running towards them, dressed in black and lime green Lycra. As she passed by, she gave Mitch a wink and a wave, which caused him to redden. This hadn't gone unnoticed by Marnie.

'Typical. She ignores me, and winks at you. And why have you gone red?'

'I haven't,' replied Mitch, unconvincingly.

Marnie screwed her eyes up and looked closely at Mitch. 'What have you been up to?'

'Nothing, Marnie. Honestly. I swear on my late mother's life.'

'Huh, well that doesn't count for much, does it? Oh well, whatever it was you did get up to, I suppose it was all for a good cause,' she said resignedly, and they both trudged back to their temporary home.

They were in the kitchen, and Mitch told Marnie what he had seen and overhead.

'What a rat!' exclaimed Marnie. 'Poor Abigail. She obviously doesn't have a clue. Talking of rats, I smell one. So, I've been invited to a "coffee afternoon" at Juliana's house. All the wives are going. Do you think it's a fishing expedition?'

'I bloody well do, Marnie, and I think you're right to smell a rat. Don't take this the wrong way, but I think they've taken you for a bit of a simpleton.'

'Excuse me! I have taken it the wrong way, but I know what you mean.' She laughed good naturedly. 'I'm just going out of curiosity, but you have no need to worry. I've been married to you long enough to have picked up a few tips, and to have a good stock of answers to any questions that may be asked. Now, what do you fancy for lunch?'

'You, Marnie. I fancy you for lunch. Now come here and let me have a nibble.'

Marnie edged closer towards him.

After lunch, Marnie changed out of her T-shirt and leggings and took a shower, not having had the time to do it before. She made an effort with her appearance adopting a smart casual look similar to Abigail's style, but not as flashy as Juliana and Svetlana, or the sporty athleisure look that Tammy and Trixie went for. Saying goodbye to Mitch, she met up with Abigail and they walked up to Juliana's house together.

'Are you ready for this?' enquired Abigail.

'Yes, I think so. Am I right in thinking I'm getting a grilling?'

Abigail smiled. 'Yes. Spot on.'

'Can I ask you something?'

'Of course you can. Ask away.'

'Don't get me wrong, Abigail, but you're not like the other wives. I've nothing against Tammy and Trixie, but the other two are a different species altogether. I clearly don't fit in here, but you do seem to have fitted in and yet you're nothing like them.'

Abigail sighed and went silent.

'I'm sorry. I shouldn't have said anything.'

'No, it's okay. I'm just thinking how to respond in a fair way. Give me a minute. Well, it's like this. When Andrew, myself and the girls, moved here, it was an upwards move from our previous home, which was in a very nice town, but with Andrew's business doing remarkably well we could afford to move somewhere that was less densely populated. We ended up here because of the proximity to a very good girls' school, the easy access to London for Andrew's work, and the fact that we are on the edge of the countryside so that there's less traffic pollution. However, moving here has been an eye-opener for me.'

'It hasn't affected Andrew as he's at work during the day, but the competition between the non-working wives, of which there are quite a few in this area, and the competitive nature of some of them, has come as a surprise to me. It's all about who goes to the best hairdresser, beauty salon, nail technician, health club and so on. It's so competitive and, as you can imagine, quite bitchy at times. Until I moved here, I wasn't even aware of this kind of lifestyle. I had a group of women friends from the girls' previous school, and they were all very down-to-earth, and very ordinary. Also, I still continued working part-time as a psychotherapist. However, since moving here, what with having to take the girls to and from school, and the various activities they do after school and at weekends, plus looking after a much larger house, there isn't much time left over for "me time". Also, with Andrew's company doing so well, he doesn't see the need for me to continue working, so I've put my career on hold for the time being.'

Marnie was taken aback by Abigail's outpouring of information. 'Oh! I didn't realise. I just thought you were one of those wives who—'

Marnie didn't get to finish her sentence because Abigail laughed out loudly. 'Never judge a book by its cover, Marnie. Before I had the girls, I had my own psychotherapy practise, and it was becoming a success. In that kind of profession, you have to be non-judgemental because your clients come to you from all kinds of different backgrounds, and with a variety of problems. Also, you have to accept people as they are, even if they are not always likeable. So, I try to treat people as I would like to be treated, and I've also taught myself to maintain an outward surface of calmness and being in control. A big "no-no", also, is becoming too emotionally involved with a client and their problems. In my profession, one has to maintain a professional and emotional distance. I've gone on a bit, haven't I?'

'No, it's okay, Abigail. It's interesting, and it's not something I've ever had experience of as I've never been in therapy, but I probably should,' replied Marnie, with a laugh.

'Anyway, in answer to your question about fitting in, the wives don't know which pigeonhole to put me in. I'm friendly towards them, and sociable, but it's from a distance. I don't compete with them, I'm not a threat, and they know this, and so I'm accepted. But I'm not part of their in-crowd, and I don't want to be. Look, I don't condone gossip, but I'll tell you something about Juliana and Svetlana which might explain their behaviour, but you must promise not to repeat it, even to Cliff.'

'I won't say anything. I promise.' Marnie had no intention of keeping what she was about to hear a secret from Mitch. Abigail didn't need to know that, though.

'Well, Juliana is Rufus' second wife. She was his secretary. Evidently, she became pregnant with their daughter while he was still married, and eventually he divorced his first wife and married Juliana. There's a saying, I don't know where it comes from, "when a man marries his mistress, it creates a vacancy".'

Abigail could see Marnie joining up the dots, and then the penny dropped. 'Are you saying that Rufus has a mistress?'

'There's another saying – "a leopard doesn't change its spots".'

'Do you know who it is?'

'I have my suspicions, but I'm not going to say anything more about that. All you need to know is that Juliana has got where she is by being manipulative, and, I suspect, ruthless. She's no angel either. Her and Rufus have an open marriage, with no questions asked, so I gather, and that way they continue to maintain their lifestyle and financial security.'

'Mm, well that's interesting. And what about Svetlana?'

Abigail chuckled. 'Sven met Svetlana when she was working as an escort.'

Marnie put her hands over her mouth in surprise, then removed them. 'You're joking! She was an escort?'

'Yes. Theirs is a marriage of convenience. Sven's only interest is the law and making as much money as possible for the company, and for himself, of course. Evidently, he has a brilliant mind and some very important clients in the shipping world who take precedence over everything. However, and I can only go on what Andrew has told me, he is not particularly interested in women, or men, for that matter, but still wants his creature comforts. A nice home, pretty wife to come back to, and sex if he feels the need. Svetlana fulfils all of this.'

'But how did he meet her?'

'Evidently, Sven goes to a lot of client functions and it's better if he has someone on his arm; you know, like "arm candy". Svetlana was one of the escorts he used, and he noticed how good she was with clients. You can see how sexy she is, and she flirts just within the bounds of acceptability. Sven realised she was an asset for him and, not surprisingly, she was very popular. Evidently, he didn't want to share her and so he married her. She makes no demands on him, as long as he provides the lifestyle she wants. Oh, and one other thing – Svetlana isn't her real name. It's Shirley.'

'What! You're joking?' said Marnie completely taken aback.

'Nope. It's true. Her real name is Shirley. Svetlana was her working name, so men thought they were hiring an exotic Russian beauty. When she married Sven, she kept her working name because it sounded good as a couple. Sven and Svetlana sounded better than Sven and Shirley. Now, that's all I'm going to say. I don't like gossip but am only telling you this so that if Juliana and Svetlana start being mean, just think about what I've told you. They've got where they are today by using their sex appeal, and probably – at least in Juliana's case – by devious means, and they aren't going to give up their hard-won wealthy lifestyle for anyone. Oh! I've been talking so much we've walked past Juliana's house.'

Marnie and Abigail turned around and walked back. The front door was open, and they went in together. 'Hello, ladies,' said Abigail cheerily, simultaneously noticing the layout of the seating arrangements. Two large settees were placed either side of the coffee table, similar to the studio layout on the set of a *Real Housewives* reunion. A solitary armchair was placed at one end of the table. Marnie had noticed the layout as well, and the word "interrogation" sprang to mind. Before Juliana could say anything, Abigail went and sat in the chair which meant that Marnie had to sit on one of the settees. She chose the one on which Tammy and Trixie sat, who both turned towards Marnie and smiled. Juliana and Svetlana, clearly flummoxed by what had just happened, fell into a momentary silence, which was filled by the assembled wives helping themselves to the tea, coffee and pastries, which were laid out on the coffee table.

The silence was broken by Juliana who came straight to the point. 'Marnie, we know so little about you and Cliff, and seeing as our husbands are thinking of investing in your husband's yacht timeshare business, we thought this would be a good opportunity to get to know you better.'

Marnie, who thought this was a fair enough comment, startled herself when she replied, 'Oh, and here's me thinking this was a wives' social get-together. Silly me. Abigail, would you mind swapping seats. If I'm going to be interrogated, let me at least sit in the chair.' Marnie was about to say "electric chair" but felt that was going a bit too far. Also, she could hear Mitch's voice in her head saying, *Careful, Marnie. Don't rub them up the wrong way. Remember, there's a lot at stake.*

Abigail got up, and swapped seats. Marnie adopted a conciliatory tone. 'I apologise. That was uncalled for. But you can see how it looks to me, can't you?'

No one answered. Some were embarrassed at being caught out; others were surprised by what appeared to be a new Marnie who was showing a spirited and confident side. The silence was broken by one of the twins' wives.

'Please don't take this the wrong way, Marnie. It's just that we haven't really got to know you that well.'

Well, whose fault is that, thought Marnie to herself.

Juliana, whose voice took on a tone softer than her usual faux posh accent, asked Marnie how she met Cliff.

Marnie was prepared for this question. 'We met on a cruise ship. I think it was the *Silver Princess*, but I can't be sure as, between us, we worked on so many over the years and were probably – as the saying goes – "ships that pass in the night".' She smiled, pleased with her cleverness.

'Oh, you worked on cruises?' said Trixie, who identified herself by her next sentence. 'Before we met

Toby and Tommy, Tammy and I thought about working on cruise ships, didn't we, Tammy?'

'Yes, Trixie, we did. But then we met the boys, and the rest is history, as they say.'

'That's a shame that you never got to try it,' said Marnie, putting on what she hoped sounded like a sympathetic voice. 'It's a wonderful life and a great way of seeing the world. Cliff and I, separately, of course, until we met each other, worked on them for many, many years.'

'What did you do?' asked Tammy.

Svetlana, who had been quiet up until now, muttered under her breath, 'I bet it wasn't in the beauty salon.' This earned a kick on the ankle from Juliana.

'No, that's right, Svetlana. It wasn't in the beauty salon.' This caused the other wives to look at Svetlana, who at least had the decency to blush at being caught out. 'I worked in hospitality, with special responsibility for the elderly guests.' Marnie had no idea if this kind of job actually existed on a cruise ship, but it sounded reasonable enough.

'Oh, so that's why you're so good with the elderly people at the care home,' chipped in Abigail. 'Marnie has become a favourite at the home. Not everyone has the patience, or the kindness that is needed.'

'What did Cliff do then?' asked Juliana, trying to steer the conversation back on course.

'He worked as a steward, and that's how he ended up doing what he does now. Over the years, he made a lot of friends on the cruise ships and some useful contacts, whom he kept in touch with. Then, when we decided to put down roots and become landlubbers,' and Marnie grinned when she said this, 'Cliff got in touch with some of them and floated the idea of staring up a yacht timeshare and brokerage business.' *Crikey,* thought Marnie, *I'm good at this. Almost as good as Mitch.*

Svetlana then asked a question which was, it seemed to Marnie, designed to throw her off guard. 'Sven and I have been on a couple of cruises. What has been your favourite place?'

Marnie put her finger to her bottom lip and tapped it. Removing her finger, she replied, 'Oh, now, let me see… It has to be Antigua. Yes, definitely Antigua.' Marnie had never been to Antigua but had read about it on the internet when she had once been researching into a possible Caribbean holiday.

'Oh, we've always wanted to go to the Caribbean, haven't we, Tammy?' said Trixie.

'Yes, and Antigua looks lovely, as does St. Lucia. Perhaps we'll get the boys to take us there on the yacht!'

'Sven and I went to Antigua one Christmas. Where did you visit then?' she asked Marnie, not to be distracted from her line of questioning.

Not to be fazed by Svetlana, Marnie smiled at her. 'What you have to understand, Svetlana, is that this was work for me and not a holiday. Even when the cruise ship docked, and everyone goes ashore for shopping and sightseeing, as employees, we still have duties to perform. I was lucky, I suppose, in that I at least got to go ashore but I still had to look after the elderly passengers I was responsible for. So, it was more of a "busman's holiday".'

'That's not what I was asking, though,' retorted Svetlana. 'I asked you where you visited in Antigua.'

Juliana shot Svetlana a warning look. 'Svetlana, Marnie is a guest here, like everyone else.'

The room went quiet again, until Marnie spoke. 'It's okay, Juliana. Svetlana is right. I digressed and didn't answer her question. I visited, along with the group I was looking after, St. John and English Harbour. Actually, I found St. John to be too busy as we weren't the only cruise ship in that day. It was quite difficult pushing a wheelchair around the capital with all the people and the traffic. English Harbour was much easier, and less busy. My second favourite place, just in case someone was going to ask that question, was Athens. We docked at Piraeus and then took an organised coach trip. Some of my group were quite happy to sit outside a café, whilst the more mobile went up to the Acropolis and I accompanied them. It was so interesting, full of history and a glimpse of Ancient Greek civilisation.' *Blimey,* thought Marnie, *where did all that come from?*

Svetlana was like a dog with a bone. She wasn't going to let go with her questions, which had taken on an interrogative tone. 'Why did you both choose this area?' she asked.

'Really, Svetlana. That's enough,' said Abigail.

Marnie held up her hand. 'It's okay, Abigail. I understand the concerns, but I thought this was supposed to be a wives' social get-together. Clearly it isn't. So, I'll be upfront with you. Cliff and I have made a lot of money over the years. You wouldn't believe the tips. The elderly American guests were great at tipping, and very generous. We didn't really have any expenses, so we accumulated quite a healthy pot of money, which we invested. By the time we decided to come ashore for good, we took the decision not to have children as we felt we had left it a bit late, and so it was just a matter of deciding where to live. As I said earlier, Cliff had made a lot of useful contacts with likeminded seafaring people who all, coincidently, lived in the south of England. And he chose to set up his business in the south. We also decided to live in a countryside location, so that we had the best of both worlds – coast and country.

'We needed somewhere with easy access to the coast, London, and one or two large towns, and we chose here. The agent told us that the house we're currently renting might be coming up for sale, which would be ideal. But you know what, I'm thinking we might have made a mistake. Cliff can run his business from anywhere and is not short of clients wanting his services.' Marnie let out a big sigh and stood up. 'So, that's my cards on the table. I'll take my leave of you now, ladies.'

She walked into the hallway, hoping and banking on the fact that the wives would imagine their yachting holidays disappearing in front of their eyes, and perhaps the husbands not being happy either. Abigail caught up with her. 'I'll come with you,' she said.

Walking down the road together, Abigail turned to Marnie. 'You did well in there. I'm impressed,' she said.

'It's all down to you, Abigail. Having you as a friend has given me confidence.' Marnie hugged Abigail and made her way home, feeling slightly downhearted as she knew they would be leaving the area soon.

Marnie found Mitch drinking tea at the kitchen table. She sat down heavily on the chair, causing Mitch to look up. 'As bad as that, was it?'

'What I need now, more than anything, is a large gin and tonic and don't go easy on the gin. Get me that, and I'll tell you everything. You won't believe it!'

Whilst Mitch was getting down a tall glass from the cupboard, and ice from the ice compartment, Marnie reflected on how far she had come from the days when she used to drink cans of ready-mixed gin and tonic. Looking up, she saw Mitch holding up two bottles of gin – one blue and one pink – and gesturing to her to choose which one.

Marnie pointed at the pink bottle. 'Pink, I think. I need something sweet after that sour experience.'

Mitch returned to the table and handed Marnie her gin and tonic. Taking a large gulp from the glass, she proceeded to fill him in.

'Crikey!' he said. 'I don't believe it. Who would have thought it? You did well in the circumstances, Marnie. How do you think it went, though?'

'Difficult to say, really. But I think we'll know soon enough. Probably after the weekend, when they've all talked it through. It's Abigail I feel sorry for, though. I'm going to miss her.'

Mitch shot Marnie a warning look. 'Marnie...'

'Yes, yes, I know. Don't get too attached.'

Unbeknownst to her, Marnie had won some respect from the women in the group. Tammy and Trixie were impressed at Marnie's handling of the situation overall, whilst Juliana was changing her opinion and now thinking that perhaps Marnie wasn't as dull and daft as she seemed. Even Svetlana was grudgingly impressed as there weren't many women, apart from Juliana, who would take her on and come out of it unscathed.

*

Although Mitch had asked the group to get back to him by the end of the week, he wasn't surprised when he hadn't heard from them because he knew they would be discussing the information gleaned by the wives on Tuesday afternoon. Thus, the weekend passed by very slowly. Ideally, Mitch would have liked to have gone away for a couple of days just to distract himself, but he knew that he had to stay put. On Monday afternoon, Marnie went to the care home as usual, and acted as she normally would when she saw Abigail. On Monday evening, the doorbell rang. It was Rufus.

'Ah, hello, Rufus. Would you like to come in and have a drink?'

'No, you're all right, Cliff. Can't stop. Juliana is serving up dinner shortly. I just wanted to get your bank details. The boys designated me the captain.' Rufus grinned when he said this. 'So, if you can let me have the necessary information, everyone will transfer the money and then presumably we will get our timeshare package.'

'Wow! That's great news, Rufus. Hold on and I'll get the bank details.' Mitch went into the living room where Marnie was watching *The One Show*. He gave a "thumbs up" sign to her, and then wrote the account details in the name of C. Mitchelson on a piece of paper.

'Here you are, Rufus. In the meantime, I'll get all the paperwork prepared and finalised from my end.'

Rufus took the piece of paper. 'Sven asked me to ask if the glossy brochure was ready yet, as he thinks he can get some of his contacts interested. However, he doesn't think the leaflet you gave us would be sufficient, because the people he has in mind would expect something a bit more professional-looking. No offence intended, Cliff.'

'No offence taken, Rufus. I agree with him. I would have much preferred to give you all something a bit glossier and impressive. I don't know what's taking the printers so long. I'll chase them up again. Tell Sven I'll drop a handful round when they're ready.'

Rufus was lingering on the doorstep.

'Is there anything else, Rufus?'

'Yes, there is, Cliff, and the matter is a bit delicate and so must stay between us. I will transfer two lots of money for two shares, but one share is to be in Andrew's name.'

Mitch put on a puzzled look, although he knew what Andrew was probably up to.

'It's like this, Cliff, old boy. Evidently, Abigail isn't keen on the idea, but Andrew is and so he's doing it behind her back. You okay with that?'

'As long as I get the money, that's all I'm interested in. Shall I give the paperwork to you then, to pass on?'

'Yes please. Now I must be going. Mustn't keep the boss waiting.'

Mitch went back into the living room. 'Right, Marnie. It's happening. We just have to be patient now and wait for the money to come in.'

By Friday, all the money was in the account. 'Right, Marnie. Get packing and be quick about it.'

'Where are we going?'

'Heathrow Airport.'

At 5am, on Saturday morning, Mitch and Marnie crept out of the house they had known as home for the past few months and put their suitcases in the boot of the rented Mercedes. Whilst Marnie was getting into the passenger seat, Mitch dropped the house keys in the letterbox. They drove away and headed for Terminal 5, Heathrow Airport, where they left the car in the long stay car park. Catching the courtesy shuttle to the terminal, they then boarded a National Express coach to Gatwick Airport. After they had checked in, and before going through departures, Mitch said he had one last thing to do. Taking an envelope out of his pocket, which was affixed with a second class stamp, he placed it in the airport post box.

'Who's that to?' asked Marnie.

'Abigail,' he replied, and Marnie knew not to ask any more questions.

*

They were seated on the plane waiting for it to depart. The pilot asked the crew to take their seats for take-off, and the plane began its taxiing along the runway. The engine noise increased and then they were in the air climbing steadily. Mitch looked out of the window, and knew that if everything went as planned, they would never set foot on British soil again. Taking hold of Marnie's hand, he lifted it to his lips and planted a kiss on it and then set it back down on her lap. A little while later, the sound of a trolley could be heard rattling down the aisle.

'I'd like a small bottle of champagne, Mitch, when the trolley comes.'

'Anything for you, my love,' he said with a smile. What he was really thinking, was *anything for a quiet life. Happy wife, happy life.*

PART FOUR

MARNIE AND MITCH

The coastline, with its sandy beach, stretched for miles, and the promenade was dotted with cafés, restaurants, shops and bars. People walked, ran and cycled. Mitch, who previously had an aversion to exercise, had bought himself a bike and found that cycling on the flat, in the sunshine, was relaxing and enjoyable. They had found themselves a small, reasonably priced, apartment to live in, in the nearest pueblo. Of course, they would have preferred to be in one of the seafront apartments, but they were much more expensive. They liked the small town though. Although they kept themselves private, they exchanged pleasantries with their neighbours so as not to appear unsociable. Marnie had found a local gym and was going there on a regular basis. Mitch had to admit that she was looking good these days. Her transformation had begun during their stay in Surrey, and she had maintained it here. Her clothes showed off her now tanned figure, rather than covering it up. She had grown her hair longer, and it was even lighter now from being in the constant sunshine.

It was late afternoon, and they had taken a walk down to the seafront and were having a drink at one of the bars. Mitch was drinking a cerveza, and Marnie was having a pina colada. He was dressed casually in white linen shorts, navy blue T-shirt, and white sliders. Marnie, on the other hand, was wearing a turquoise-coloured figure-hugging sundress, with a yellow flower pattern, and in her newly pierced ears she wore the earrings that Mitch had given her, which used to belong to Fiona. She hadn't managed to get a replacement engagement ring, but she was no longer bothered because she was hatching a plan.

The fact that Marnie hadn't pressured Mitch into buying a replacement ring, together with the fact that she no longer wore her wedding ring, which Mitch had noticed, prompted him to ask what she was up to. She had smiled sweetly at him, and explained that she was happy with the earrings, and that her wedding ring was now too loose and she had taken it off because she didn't want to lose it. Although he accepted the explanation, he suspected that she was up to something. There was something else as well he had noticed. For the walk down to the seafront, she had worn flat sandals. However, once seated, she now took a pair of yellow stiletto shoes out of her large handbag and put them on.

'Why are you all dolled up? We're only having an early evening drink, and then it's back to the apartment.'

'I'm going out,' answered Marnie.

'What do you mean, you're going out? Where are you going, and who are you going with?'

'That's for me to know, and for you not to know,' she laughingly replied, echoing words Mitch had once said to her.

'Marnie…' Mitch gave her a warning look. 'Don't try to be clever.'

'I'm going out for dinner with Reginald.'

'Who the fuck is Reginald?'

'Now, now, Mitch. Watch your language. You don't need to worry.'

'I want to know who this Reginald character is, who's taking *my wife* out to dinner.'

'Reginald is someone I met at the gym…'

'Oh, so that's why you've been going there a lot – to see your fancy man!'

'He's 75, for heaven's sake! And he's lonely. Him and his wife bought a villa and moved out here. Sadly, his wife died and now he lives alone.'

'How come you got chatting with him, anyway?'

'He was on the treadmill…'

Mitch gave a big sigh. 'My life is one long treadmill.'

'Shut up, Mitch. As I was saying, he was on the treadmill and he couldn't get it to start, so I helped him.'

'I bet you did. I bet you pressed all the right buttons.'

'There's no need to be vulgar. I helped him choose the right programme, and we got talking, and then we started having coffee together afterwards. Anyway, you're always out on your bike, so what's the problem?'

Mitch had gone into one of his sulks.

'Please don't sulk. Look, all those times I had to accept that you were seeing and talking to other women, and I never made a fuss. Now it's my time to have some fun.'

'It wasn't fun. It was work.'

'Yeah, and my name is Rudolph, and I can hear bells jingling. Right, I'm off. He's collecting me in his car just up the road.'

Marnie got up and walked away. After a few minutes, Mitch also got up and followed discreetly behind her. An old dark blue Rolls Royce was parked at the kerbside. Mitch stared open-mouthed when Marnie got into the car and gave the elderly driver a quick peck on the cheek. *Well, blow me down*, he thought, *I've trained her well*, impressed that the car was a Rolls Royce.

EDITH

Although Edith could look back on the extraordinary events she had become involved in, and chastise herself for being so gullible, she nevertheless still relived the feelings of excitement and nervous anticipation which had made her dull uneventful life come alive. She remembered how happy she had felt, and still occasionally touched her lips where a stranger had planted a kiss on them. She still felt a tingle and a thrill at this memory, which is why she went back on the dating website to see if Lionel was still online. He was. Edith wasted no time, and contacted him, which is why she found herself sitting on a bench on Worthing seafront, next to Lionel. They were both eating an ice cream and getting to know one another better. After they had finished, Lionel stood up and asked Edith if she would like to go for a walk.

'Yes please,' she had replied.

'Will you take my arm then, Edith, dearest?' he had said.

'Yes, I think I will, Lionel,' She reached up and gave him a kiss on the cheek.

ABIGAIL

The men who lived at the top end of Green Park Road were in shock, and busy making phone calls to their banks to try and get their money back and attempt to trace where it had gone to. They realised they had been the victim of a clever scam when no timeshare certificates or paperwork of any kind had arrived in their mailboxes. Rufus, who had been designated the leader of the group, had gone round to the house where Cliff – as he had known him – and Marnie had lived, to find that no one was at home. He tried a couple of more times, thinking that perhaps they were away on holiday, but finally came to the conclusion that they no longer lived there. He went to see Abigail, who was the designated person to welcome new people to the neighbourhood, to find out which agent they had rented the house from.

Having got the details, he paid a visit to the estate agent who had expressed surprise at Rufus' visit, as he didn't know that the house was empty. He suggested that they might have gone on holiday but revealed to Rufus that they were behind with the rent. Rufus then told the agent the whole story. At this point, the estate agent remembered that he had never heard back from the referees, but he didn't tell Rufus this in case he was in anyway held liable for the events that had ensued. Rufus and the agent decided to go to the house together, and it was as Rufus suspected. On opening the letterbox with the spare set of keys kept by the agent, to see if there was any mail which might indicate where the Mitchelsons had gone, they found the house keys. On entering the house, they were struck by the silence. Walking through the rooms, there was no sign of anyone having lived there. So now Rufus had the unenviable task of letting the others have the bad news.

Abigail wasn't concerned by any of this, because Andrew had told her that he wasn't investing in Cliff's timeshare scheme, and she believed him. In any event, she had other more pressing things on her mind. An envelope addressed to her had arrived with the words "Personal and Private" written in the top left-hand corner. She had opened it up to find a sheet of white paper on which was typed the following words: *Dear Abigail, Firstly, sorry. Nothing personal. Secondly, ask Andrew why he was not on the yacht with everyone else, and who was the woman he was with in the woods on his day off. Cliff.*
PS: Marnie sends her love.

MARNIE AND MITCH

Marnie and Mitch were having lunch al fresco. Marnie looked at Mitch and smiled at him. Taking hold of his left hand, she said, 'You know I do love you, don't you?'

Mitch was immediately suspicious. *What's she after*, he thought. 'What are you after?' he said.

'Can you let me have your wedding ring please?'

Mitch, who was just about to pop a cherry tomato into his mouth, held it in mid-air. 'Why do you want my wedding ring? What are you up to?'

'I'm getting married.'

Mitch put the tomato back down on his plate. 'But you're married to me!' he said, somewhat hurt.

'I know I am. Just listen. Reginald is loaded. He lives in this huge villa all by himself, and he needs looking after. He asked me if I would ever consider getting married again.'

Mitch was puzzled. 'What do you mean, "getting married again"? You're still married. He does know that, doesn't he?'

Marnie chewed her lip and looked sheepish. 'He thinks I'm divorced.'

'What!'

'He thinks I'm divorced, and that I live alone. So, I'm going to suggest to him that I move into the villa with him and care for him, but that we would have to be married as I have my reputation to think of. That's why I need your ring. I can present it to him and say that, if he's really serious about us getting married, then I have already bought the ring and we can marry immediately.'

Mitch looked sad and bewildered. 'But where does that leave me, Marnie? What will I do without you?'

'Don't be silly. You'll follow on shortly after the wedding. Reginald admits that he doesn't like driving now, and I've persuaded him to get a driver. Also, the villa needs a bit of a spruce up. He's let it go a bit. There's the pool that needs regular cleaning, and the garden needs tidying up, and so I suggested that we should look for a general handyman-cum-driver. That's where you come in. I'll tell him that I've advertised, then I will interview you and give you the job. Then I'll introduce you to Reginald. You can also live-in, as the villa has an annexe which is used as a storeroom at present but can easily be cleared out and decorated. What do you think? You can still do your online scamming when we don't need you to drive us anywhere, but you won't have to worry about a thing and, of course, we will still see each other on a daily basis. Oh, and I'll be able to sneak out when Reginald is asleep for a bit of "you know what"! Isn't it exciting? I can't wait.' She rubbed her hands together gleefully.

With this new set of circumstances, Mitch wasn't sure if he'd gone up or down in the world, but it all sounded good to him. As long as he could still keep his hand in with his online romance cons, and now with Marnie's imminent marriage to Reginald meaning he would have a new surname to play with, he could cope with the rest. Also, he had no doubt in his mind that Marnie had a plan – after all, she had been taught by the best teacher – and so he handed over his wedding ring.

Later that night, whereas Marnie was in a deep sleep, Mitch was wide awake. Disjointed thoughts were filling his brain. Marnie had said she had stopped wearing her wedding ring because it was too loose. She had been going to the gym and had met Reginald. It was very convenient, then, that she wasn't wearing her ring because she had told Reginald she was divorced. Mitch knew that this was all somehow linked but couldn't quite sort it out in his head. He finally fell asleep with the thought that Marnie had very cleverly turned the tables on him and conned both him and Reginald. He then realised that he had taught her too well.

TWO WOMEN

Two women, who did not know each other, walked into Brighton Police Station at the same time, and sat down in the waiting area, one chair apart, until the duty sergeant became available. The person currently reporting something was taking ages, and twenty minutes had already passed.

'I wonder what's taking so long?' said the older woman. 'I wish I'd brought Georgie with me now, instead of leaving him at home.'

'Is that your husband?' asked the younger woman.

The older woman laughed. 'No, Georgie's my dog. I named him after my husband, George. Now there was a decent and honest man,' she reminisced. 'What you saw, is what you got. Not like some of the men these days.'

They sat in silence for a few minutes more, and then the younger woman asked the older woman what she was reporting.

'I was the victim of a con man.'

'Oh, me too!'

'It was my fault, though. I was completely taken in by him. He seemed very nice on the surface. Dressed nicely, was charming, and, I must say, he was not bad-looking either.' She smiled at the memory. 'He was my lodger. The thing is, he was also very clever. He never actually asked me for any money. I gladly offered it to him and wouldn't take no for an answer. Yes, Daniel was a very clever con man indeed.'

'Did you say his name was Daniel?'

'Yes, Daniel Simpson.'

Fiona frowned. *It must be the same person*, she thought. *It can't be a coincidence.* Also, Dan, as she had known him, never asked her for money either. She had offered it. 'Your name isn't Mrs Baxter, by any chance, is it?'

'No, dear. It's Beresford. Dorothy Beresford.'

'Hello, Dorothy.' She shook Dorothy's hand. 'My name is Fiona, and I was also conned by a very charming and good-looking man called Daniel Simpson. Sounds to me as if we were conned by the same person, doesn't it?'

The duty sergeant became free, and both women went up to the counter together to report that they had been the victim of a con man called Daniel Simpson.

THE END

CPSIA information can be obtained
at www.ICGtesting.com
Printed in the USA
LVHW111146170822
726111LV00005B/162